ABE LINCOLN'S MISFITS

By

MJ Politis, Ph.D.

276 5th Avenue Suite 704 #944
New York, NY 10001

Copyright © April 12, 2023 M. J. Politis

ISBN (Paperback): 978-1-918002-68-3
ISBN (Hardback): 978-1-918002-69-0
ISBN (eBook): 978-1-918002-70-6

Cover Design by Woodbridge Publishers.

Find out more about our upcoming releases and authors at www.woodbridgepublishers.com and sign up for our newsletter to stay updated!

Dedicated to you…the reader. With appreciation for
your being open to this offering.

And all those I have known who made this offering
possible.

CHAPTER 1

John Smith's life was as generic, boring, and predictably middle-American as his name in Pleasanton County, Iowa. Indeed, Pleasanton's flat fields of corn, wheat, and barley that went as far as the eye could see were as plentiful in 1936 as they had been 2 decades ago. Mother Nature had spared the God-fearing and flag-loving citizens the wrath of the Dust Bowl, which turned most of the crop and grass-bearing soil in America into a dust bowl. It had been spared Indian raids five decades earlier. The once proud, well-fed, and nomadic tribes had abandoned the buffalo-depleted land that was then made to bleed with the plow soon after the first sodbusters arrived. The blood from their plows and metal spades provided the pale-skinned residents and their progeny with stabilized prosperity each year. It provided them with everything they needed and most of what they wanted in a (relative to anywhere else anyway) crime-free paradise with fluctuations that were as flat as the plain Jane pancakes they ate for breakfast and the hill-free horizons that boxed you in comfortably in all directions.

As for John Smith's role in maintaining this 'going nowhere but not wanting to anyway' Paradise, he was promoted at the age of 25 to Chief Regional Operating officer for the Iowa State Insurance Company. He had a ten-year track record of selling more policies than any other agent for three hundred miles in any direction. The company had to pay out fewer policies for 'accidents' caused by Nature or the hand of man (and woman) than any other agent in Iowa, for which he was generously rewarded by the Head Office.

With that (as Preacher Johnson said, anyway) 'God-given' prosperity, John was able to finally woo to the alter Thelma, the prettiest girl in his High School class. He had yearned for her affection since he was able to spout pubic hair on his family jewels and peach fuzz on his upper lip. After spawning his eldest son, averagely handsome on a good day and in the right light Jake, by 'accident', Thelma provided the Smith household with two daughters, Rachel and Agnes.

On this day of October 5, 1936, John left the office at 5 pm, as scheduled, clad in his plain brown suit, which never acquired wrinkles, and a black tie that made his white shirt seem darker to the soul. As was his trademark, he departed with polite and perhaps respectful nods from his less-than-successful and mostly older subordinates. But John was contemplating what surprises his wife and children would provide for him for his birthday at home. The big 40! A landmark, he reluctantly and unexpectedly found himself thinking and feeling as if half of his life was over. But there was another half to make something of, for himself, his family, or…the world. A world that was in turmoil and transition, according to the headline on the newspaper he read from his always reserved for him and freshly cleaned seat on the bus going home.

"Spain is in an uproar again? A civil war starting there?" Paul Williamson noted from the driver's seat in the rearview mirror, reading the headline in the specially ordered newspaper John had opened up, and hiding inside. "And who is this General Franco? Is he with them or with us, as Americans, that is?"

"Hard to say, Paul," John noted, reading between the lines to smell out the real agenda of the writer and the newspaper owner within the article about the Civil War in Spain. On one side, there was the democratically elected as well as people serving Republicans backed ONLY by Soviet Russia. On the other side, rich aristocrats, the Catholic Church, along with the Army led by Franco, now got tons of active support from Nazi Germany and Fascist Italy. "But someone here should do something about the War that is killing far more innocent civilians than armed soldiers," he commented, seeing below the article that the American Congress had just elected to join the rest of the Capitalist 'democratic' countries in the world to ban all exports of any supplies, or people, to the Republicans and their Russian allies.

"Why should WE do anything about it?" Paul inquired regarding the War that had officially broken out four months ago. "There's a big ocean 'tween them and us," he continued. "Right folks?" he inquired of the other passengers, who responded with an overwhelming barrage of 'yeps,' 'You said it, Paul,' and 'That's God's honest truth.'

"And an ocean of flat land the winners or losers in this new war have to cross if they want to invade us here, which will kill them with boredom," John thought, but dared not say, as his social position and welfare of his family depended on him being 'predictably middle American.'

"But one thing about what's goin' on in Spain," Paul added. "Let them Mexican speakin' Spaniards, Reds, and Sieg Heiling Huns keep the Spanish flu on their side of the Atlantic. Each one of us lost a friend or family member to that influenza. Which none of us woulda got if Europers stayed in Europe and our troops stayed at home like they were supposed ta."

Once again, John, who had committed the primal sin in Pleasanton to get a free-thinking college education for two years anyway, took in a deep breath. Through tight lips, he held back the fire he wanted to unleash upon his fellow passengers. Who accepted ignorance as truth from the master mechanic and unelected Mayor Paul, and who kept his position of power and influence somehow by NOT aspiring to get any titles.

So, as usual, John retreated into and found painful solace within, involuntarily and 'accidentally' acquired regret. He self-observed himself, glancing down at his feet, noting his tight-fitting polished business shoes. He recalled the time he wore loose, scruffed, real horse cowboy boots. Then he looked out the window at fenced-in pasture horses as they chased each other in a game invented by themselves, for themselves. Such reminded him of the days when he had ridden in the local beans and bacon rodeo circuit and on the more open range. They were the good old days before 'settling in' to being a better-paid professional who got his pick of what steaks he could eat as many times a day as he desired. And to become a responsible husband, father, and American, taking care of family and country first, second and last.

John's eyeline was drawn to the photo in the newspaper of the latest victims in the Spanish Civil War. Such reminded him of the stories his father wrote back from Europe before he died in the War to End All Wars in the trenches. A father whose body was never recovered. A father who made John promise and solemn pledge to 'stay at home and live responsibly.' Because 'an educated angel like you, John, could never become a devil. Or a man who survives the kind of hell that only the sinful and ignorant of us deserve to be thrown into.'

John's assessment of himself plummeted at he noted the time, 5:15. It was the hour of his birth 40 long years ago. "What did I not do, and what did I do out of cowardice or ignorance?" He asked himself. The inability to answer that question, or correct it, was only amplified by the citizenry on the bus whose bodies, bellies, and material (but not spiritual) needs he had looked after broke out into 'Happy Birthday,' after which they gave him a gift. It was a plaque with his face on it, featuring 'Pleasanton's Most Solid Citizen' in the most generic, expressionless black print available. It was signed by what seemed to be almost everyone in town, with handwriting that was…generically flawless and soul-less.

John smiled with gratitude, of course. He thanked everyone as he emerged from the bus, then stroked his perfectly combed hair and felt his cleanly shaved face. Such had a covering of short 8-hour-old stubble on it, which felt like a layer of thumbtacks to his fingertips. He walked cautiously towards the door to his house, a two-story brick structure that had survived 50 years of weather challenges from Mother Nature.

But the sun was setting, and he had to face the light of day inside. He carefully and, as quietly as possible opened the door; as predicted, his family was there, singing Happy Birthday. Rachel and Agnes emitted the song with lovingly angelic voices accompanied by smiles framed by long blonde hair flowing down past their shoulders. His wife, Thelma, was the cake holder. With a stylish bob and the dress she first wore on the night of their engagement, she seemed in the light of the candles to be a still pretty 24-year-old farm girl. Inwardly, John sensed that she was an 82 years tired and non-expressive old maid. Which one she was depended on how you looked at her. Yet her voice was…pleasant and, in its own limited way, loving. As for John's son Jake, his face was tense, his smile forced. His 18-year-old eyes said something his mouth was not as he sang Happy Birthday in off-key tones that felt more like a dirge.

At the conclusion of the (some would say anyway) free home concert, John blew out the candles. He felt a heaviness in his chest, then emitted a cough.

"Are you alright?" Thelma asked, gently caressing John's back. "You aren't smoking again, are you?"

"No," John said, finding no reason to hide the truth.

"So, what are you going to do about that cough!" Thelma insisted.

"And this," Jake whispered into John's ear, pointing to the newspaper featuring stories about the Spanish 'situation.'

John gazed at and into Jake's soul, engaging more deeply into the unspoken conversation which John had welcomed, then had halted, so many times.

"What I, and we, have to, I suppose," John said to John in words.

"Huh?" John's two girls muttered in unison.

"What are you talking about, John?" Thelma demanded to know.

John was silent. Thelma turned to Jake, punching him gently in the chest. "Come on, talk! I have ways of making you talk!" she said, imitating a German interrogator she had seen in a recent play about The Great War at the Des Moines theatre.

John felt his lips turn upward, his eyes opening up, his face feeling less tight as he observed Thelma being…expressive and artistic. And filled with humorous Life and Vitality. Finally! After all those years of losing or forfeiting, the ability to be Alive is a big A. But it was too little and too late.

"I have to go out," John said after a long reflective pause, looking downward so that what he was really meaning would not be understood. "Some work I have to do that I forgot about," he continued as he walked into his study. "I won't be long. Really," he promised as he closed the door behind him.

He gazed at the exit door from the study. It led to open air when he needed a smoke break or a midnight ride that the doctors said was not good for his health. But John could hear all too painfully the interrogation Thelma, then the girls, gave to Jake. "Dad has some important out-of-town business he has to attend to, which he's doing, finally, for us!" John could hear Jake say. "He'll be back soon."

"When?" Thelma inquired.

As John exited the study and mounted the horse that would take him to the train station and perhaps to Madrid (if he could get on the right boat and in the right Socialist freedom-fighting company in New York), he imagined what Jake would say to stall his well-meaning inquisitors. He hoped that Jake would make the right decision for himself as to whether he would value family or the world or somehow balance those two so often conflicting loyalties. Whatever that was.

CHAPTER 2

Tim 'don't call me Timothy' Jackson planted his blister-covered soles and frostbitten heels on the pavement on 7th Avenue, yet as the door behind him was about to slam shut yet one more time. "Damn Nigger sharecroppers, they should shuffle on back ta Alabama, don't ya know," he heard from the Irish Foreman through the crack in the window at the Williamson Metal and Lumber Supply company. The Foreman's face was the snow-white face. It cracked into a cold smile after informing Jackson that the ten slots for workers that had been open as many minutes ago had just been filled.

"Or better yet, we should send them back to Africa," came from an Ivy League Southern 'gentleman' in a three-piece suit that was never once soiled by factory soot or sawdust. He sounded very much like President Woodrow Wilson, champion of the League of Nations and active supporter against any Negro from bearing arms, even while doing service in the US Army during the Great War. After all, the intelligence of the Negroid race was better suited for shoveling dirt, carrying sandbags, and fetching water.

The industrial 'gentleman' looked downward from his wire-rim glasses through the frosted window directly at Tim with an upturned, cleanly shaven, chiseled chin. "Yes, we should perhaps send ALL of them back to Africa. Particularly the upstart ingrateful Darkies who don't know the place we and God intended for them to stay in. And as for the ones who want to be labor and civil rights organizers who are working for Red godless Soviet devils in Moscow," the establishment owner pontificated, fully aware that Tim Jackson was eavesdropping without permission, hanging offense in 'respectable' towns. He edged his manicured index finger across his neck, indicating what would happen if Tim did not heed the 'kind' warning.

Tim could have answered back with a defiant gesture of his own. With a third-digit salute, a clenched fist, or a political retort that was far more expressive and elegantly biting. But he was interrupted from doing so by the rumbling of his empty stomach. It had not experienced food other than the scant findings one found in dumpsters for at least three days. And well-fed Cops five years younger than him, in bright blue uniforms who motioned for him to 'go on home, boy' at each 'Dumpster Diner.' Such was a request he would have gladly complied with IF he still had a house, shack, or corner of a broken-down boarding house he could call home.

Tim hesitated, contemplating his options. He looked North towards Harlem, recalling the twenty establishments with help wanted signs that were reserved for 'others.' Then West, towards the Bowery, where he had tried unsuccessfully on his 'best behavior' to seek employment in the lowest paying jobs available, or creatable. Then South, which, beyond the Statue of Liberty, still lay the Dixie states, where he had an estranged and crazy (legally anyway) wife and two children who she said were his, but he knew wasn't. Then, to the East, considering how he could hitch a ride across the river and stow away on a boat to Russia, perhaps. Or at least to France, where, back in 1917, General Pershing had 'given him away' to the French commanders. Who gave him a real gun to kill Germans instead of a shovel to dig latrines, trenches, and wells for White soldiers? And the opportunity to fight and be respected by his 'Paleface' French comrades as a fellow soldier fighting oppression and to be an effective defender of both French and American democracy. Tim reached into his pocket, pulling out the medals of honor the Parisian generals had given him for heroism. Considered showing them to the cops in front of him and to 'Mister Williamson' on the other side of the closed window.

"Who'd ya steal those medals from, boy?" the 'elder' Cop, whose upper lip had a real rather than peach fuzz mustache, bellowed out from his oversized belly with a half Irish and half New Yawk drawl. The junior patrolman next to him whipped out his billiclub, pounding it on his palm.

"They're mine!" Tim proclaimed.

"And what else do ya have in that pocket, boy!" the senior patrolman demanded to know. "Some money I'm hopin'," he continued, slipping into an Irish accent. "Otherwise," he said, turning to his 'student.' "What's the punishment for vagrancy?"

"Thoytie days in da big house," the junior 'officer' replied in American-born Brooklynese. "Hard labor, so ya can learn about honest work."

"And six months if'n ya don't see the wisdom in that, ya Darkie Hobo piece of---" the senior Cop mockingly blasted out of his fat lips with a breath reeking of whiskey, racial hatred, and actively maintaining ignorance.

Curtailing another set of descriptors that Tim had heard before from lynch rope-bearing yahoos in Mississippi and landlords of White Only neighborhoods in Yankee New York, Tim pulled out a watch from his pocket. "My grandfather's timepiece, in synch with the rhythm of and honoring the Greek god Chronos. Imparted to me prior to my departure to engender battle in the well-intended, unfortunately failed War to End All Wars in 1917. It's worth at least twenty dollars," he said, still confining his anger into pragmatic yet dignified respect for himself and whatever honor could exist in the law somewhere. "And as my still lucid cerebral faculties recall, the fee to avert incarceration for vagrancy is ten dollars."

Tim knew that half of the 'woyds' he had told the Cops were beyond their 'vocabulary.' He indulged in a moment of vengeful delight at their confusion as to his verbiage. He reflected on his self-educated Grandfather's words when sending him off to War. That 'an education is something they can never take away from you,' especially if it is self-taught. And, of course, that 'the price of being educated was to be on the shitlist of the ignorant.' It was proven by Grandpa delivering those lines from the end of a rope when he was lynched for daring to politely correct a Southern Belle's Shakespear quote on the streets of Birmingham, Alabama. He had dared as well to look her in the eye while she was having a PMS attack.

Finally, the overly armed Cops made a decision. "We'll be takin' that watch now," the senior Patrolman declared, motioning with his hands to hand it over. "Unless ya got twenty dollars in real money."

"Which I don't have, in real money," Tim replied, for the moment. Chose not to challenge the 'just got word from headquarters this morning' change in the law regarding how much money one is supposed to have to not be a vagrant. "Half of the city is out of work! And poverty is NOT a crime. It's a disease, spread by---"

"---We'll take the watch now, then," the older Cop interjected. "As collateral," he said as his partner in slime edged his fingers on the handle of his pistol. "Or it's the big house for you! And the laws and sentences for vagrancy and sedition are gettin' harder each day, Comrade."

It was a matter of fists against guns, yet again. Tim's stomach churned, not only out of hunger but indignation. He recalled a book written about working and looking for honest (and dignified, if possible) work by a White Scholar translated from Russian about the French Revolution and the 'workers riots' against the Czar in his homeland. "You keep people hungry for supper; they'll beg for food. And the peasants will do your bidding as slaves. You starve them, and they will revolt," he recalled. "But only if you don't wait too long," he remembered from observing and nearly experiencing himself, that even a dedicated soul can't raise a gun, pitchfork, or fist against an oppressor if his body is starved to the point of being nothing but flabby skin and fragile bones.

Noting that he was getting no help from any of the bystanders on the street and a nod of 'if you know what is good for you, boy' from 'Professor' Williamson, Tim handed over the watch. "We'll be holdin' on to this for ya, Comrade," the Dublin-born and American-raised Cop promised with a gleam in his eye, knowing that he could get a lot more from a pawn shop for it than twenty dollars. "And we'd be wantin' that medal as well, which is worth---"

"---Nothing, in cash anyway," Tim interjected, out of turn, a punishable offense to a White Sheriff in Alabama as well as a Caucasian Cop in New York. "I tried to get something for it many times to feed my wife, my kids, and…" Tim felt himself to be a failure, yet again. This time, with no chance of getting back up again after being shut down. The Cops saw the defeat in his bowed head as they smirked victory with their fat lips,

"God be with ya, son," the Irish Cop said to Tim, laying his grubby hand on the WWI veteran's shaking shoulder. It felt like a rock penetrating into his bones. "And God bless America," his underling added, plummeting that sharp stone into the depths of Tim's soul.

As New York's Finest moved on to harass others who didn't fit into or threatened the American Capitalistic and Imperialistic dream, Tim considered that issue of God. The Spirit big S he still somehow wanted, and needed, to believe in but now couldn't. Still, he prayed for an answer to his dilemma and that of the world. What was to happen to his kids at home, his crazy 'wife,' and the other misfits and unfortunates roaming the streets looking for work and purpose?

And was it a misfortune to finally encroach upon the soul-dead Cops and their White bosses?

"Gotta give me somethin' to make it right," Tim said to the Deity upstairs as he looked up to the blue sky. Grey snow began to fall from clouds in preparation to dump more 'crystal white shit' over his roofless head and life. "Or at least tell me a way to fight against it, even if I die in the---"he muttered regarding the curse inflected on the bulk of humanity after the Big Crash on Wall Street; he lowered his head, causing him to fall to the ground, bringing the contents of a garbage bin in front of him with him. His eyes meet with a crumbled and, apparently, blood-stained pamphlet. "The Communist Party needs YOU to fight Fascism in Spain, so it doesn't come here," it said in bold red letters. The call to arms was complimented by even bolder and inspirationally hopeful artwork of workers like himself, whose skin was not all white. All of the people portrayed had clenched fists but kind and caring faces. He turned the leaflet around, eagerly reading the description on the back. He ignored, for now, the rancid pieces of bread which was embedded with the rest of the trash. The menu on the entre to feed the soul indeed was mouth-watering.

"Democratic-Republican Spain, what is left of it anyway," the discourse in bold print related. "Where land was given back to the Peasants. Where workers get paid fair wages, and everyone gets a chance to do dignified work, where each gives according to their ability and takes according to their needs. Where everyone works and everyone eats. Where everyone gets health care for free, according to need. Where there is no racism. Where each man, woman, and child has his own relationship with God without the rich Priests who allow the poor to die of poverty, disease, and hunger telling you what it is. Where there is universal education for everyone." The last item on the menu made Tim scratch his head in retort. "And where women get the vote?" he read. "Even crazy women like me, wife?" he asked the image of the Worker Comrade leader on the front of the pamphlet. "But," he reasoned upon reflection of the matter regarding the woman he hated, pitied, yet still felt responsible for, no matter how often she cheated on and degraded him. "If she gets free health care, that maybe can take care of the crazy and maybe the rest of it."

Tim Jackson was a philosophical pragmatist. Every problem he faced, HAD to have a solution. And every new idea had to have a way to be implemented somehow. His tenacity and prayers were answered when his eyes met the bottom of the political menu. "Volunteers needed to fight the German and Italian Fascists so the cancer of oppression doesn't spread!"

Tim recalled his own stake in this. How fellow 'Darkie' Jesse Owens was denied the Gold Medal in the 1936 Olympics because Hitler didn't want to give it to a member of the 'Inferior Races.' And there was the matter of the German Jews, including Albert Einstein, as well as those with other brands of heart and mind intelligence. They had escaped their homeland with horror stories about what was happening there. The reports were ignored, ridiculed, or dismissed as Bolshevic propaganda by Americans, mostly white ones. Many of them, not surprisingly, were still doing business with Mussolini and Hitler. Those 'God-fearing' Americans branded the Socialist Experiments in Spain and Russia as 'demonic events run by Godless Communists and Jews'. Jews who, in Tim's experience after seeking work and purpose in New York, were more religious, humanitarian, and intelligent than most Christians.

As the first snowflakes came down, turning into snowballs faster than you could say or sing, 'Paul Robson,' Tim worked his way to the Communist Party Office. It was shared with the Workers Unions and the ACLU which, hopefully, was still intact.

CHAPTER 3

The recruitment room for volunteers to fight for democracy abroad, and therefore at home, reeked of borscht, Polish sausages, and stale cabbage, along with a plethora of other smells from kitchens Vincent DeAngelo had never experienced in Little Italy in Manhattan or the old country. But in the age of soup lines outside that served re-boiled for the fifth time chicken bones served with three-day-old white bread with a slab of meat perhaps of animal or maybe human origin, it was a refreshing ill-defined harmony of aromas.

The international working man's 'Commie-Unionist-Anarchist' cuisine was served by long-haired maidens with slender physiques, which were more about 'girlish figures' than underfed bellies. Certainly, it was a feast for the eyes, relative to the plain-Jane, by choice, Salvation Army women serving bread and (as they said anyway) beef bologna to the hungry on the soup lines outside of St. Boniface's church. Or the soon-to-be fat-assed and thunder-thighed vagina-bearing bobbed counter help in Uncle Sal's bakery around the corner who sold cannolis and spumoni instead of merely bread and milk to 'special customers.' And, of course, to selected passion working stiffs who didn't ask any questions about why there was so much money in the secret compartment within the till and so few customers supplying it.

Vincent's studly 20-year-old brown eyes still lingered on the sturdy as a rock but beautiful as a summer rose Slavic chow vendor who had served him lunch. They exchanged unspoken propositions and proposals to her that went well beyond 'How you like the perogies, Comrade?'. After all, they were the right fit biologically. Vincent's long arms and legs were attached to a set of muscles that made him look like a Greek god. His face had grown within the last two years into features that made him handsome to the naked eye. It was told by several envious fats, double-chinned, large-nosed Jewish producers on Broadway; it was the kind of mug that would make any woman seeing it on screen wet her panties. As for Comrade Natasha, who introduced herself to Vincent with the little English she knew, she seemed to be the kind of 25-year-old babe who would never lose her looks, charm, or skills in the bedroom. No, Natasha would never be like the girls in Vincent's neighborhood who had lost, or forfeited, the aforementioned by the time they had their third kid or were desperately hanging on to their fourth pimp.

Just when Vincent was about to close the deal with that 'yes!' smile. It complemented his perfectly trimmed 'just thick enough but not too bushy' mustache; a man on the opposite side of the desk interrupted his gustatory and visual pleasure fest... "She's married," Robert Feinstein said.

"So why doesn't she have a wedding ring around her finger?" Vincent challenged.

"Because she's married to the Cause," the acclaimed, solidly Jewish, and proclaimed atheist writer countered with a stern, frozen face colder than any Cosa Nostra Don that Vincent had ever encountered. Adding to the contradictions which seemed to be embellishing the day, this famous freedom fighter anarchist who seemed to be making rules for everyone in the joint looked more like a WASP Captain in a Cavalry Beats the Injuns film. In the right light, and when he turned his head just the right way, he resembled Custer without the mustache or fringed coat. Or a godfather of some other kind of Mob. "Yeah, Natasha's married to the Cause," Robert added, this time as an older brother trying to keep the genetic lines of his clan from being contaminated by 'impure' blood.

"Which I am, ya know," Vincent acknowledged, for now anyway, seeing and grasping for the opportunity of the moment. Experiencing for the first time a merging of agendas with no conflicting loyalties, for reasons he dared not tell 'Captain Comrade Robert, or perhaps even Major Natasha, why. The Sicilian-born American, whose usefulness to anyone was more between his ears than below his neck, took a quick, and hopefully unnoticed, glance at the posters plastered around the room. They bore hammers, sickles, and 'common folk' handling such with the kind of pride Vincent seldom saw on the wage slaves who didn't have the luck or smarts to be a member of a Mob family.

Vincent saw in the faces of the rebels in print, as well as the organizers of the joint, a new brand of power and confidence. Their eyes revealed not an ounce of fear and more pounds of heroic pride than any recruiting poster Vincent recalled seeing in any war museum. Or on the faces of any Americans in the parades going through Little Italy who had defended the stars and stripes in the Wars against the Confederacy, the Spanish Colonialists in 1898, and the Kaiser back in 1918. Or the 'we got em good' mugs on the paintings of the Garibaldi Italians who kicked the Austrians and the aristocratic petty royalty out of their country eighty years ago, which were on every wall of every house Vincent grew up in.

"I'm a Fascist fighting Working man!" Vincent proclaimed into Robert's WASP face with a clenched right fist, keeping his own reason for coming into the building during the recruitment lunch to himself. "Fighting for freedom of all Workers everywhere!" he continued, looking into peasant-princess Natasha's welcoming eyes.

"Whose hands have no callouses or blisters on them," Robert noted, pointing to Vincent's open left hand. "And whose hands, perhaps…" he continued, looking at the questionnaire Vincent had filled out and signed. "Are dirty in other ways?"

Robert related the comments, and perhaps more, to Natasha in a language Vincent didn't recognize. The glow in her face turned into dark, solemn despair, then anger. She channeled her indignation and disappointment into her task as a dispenser of food and literature to the long line of new possible recruits to the Cause. She slapped the free food into the bowls rather than laying them with a musical movement of the spatula.

"Whatever he said, it ain't true!" Vincent yelled out to Natasha. Then, to anyone else who would listen. Robert passed the questionnaire Vincent had filled out to a short, stocky woman walking with a limp. She had thin white hair and scalp wounds, with scars on her once young, beautiful face. She related relating something to Natasha in Spanish which led to her motioning with her arthritic index finger a big red X on Vincent's application to join the Cause. "I got as much right to fight Fascist bastards as anyone else here! And more motivation!" Vincent barked at the young Feinstein.

"To escape jail here?" the old woman forced through a disfigured mouth containing less than half the teeth she had once had. "Or somehow find a better life on a battlefield abroad after losing a war with a woman you loved here?"

"Or that you're trying to prove to your family, father, dead ancestor, sweetheart, or yourself that you're a hero!" Robert added. "Who---."

"-- has as much love of freedom and hatred of Fascism than anyone here!" Vincent yelled into Robert's face at the top of his lungs. "Even her!" he continued, pointing to the woman. "Especially after what they did to my family back in the old country!"

"Your family in Ethiopia, where Mussolini and massacred tens of thousands of innocent people?" Robert inquired with a condescending smirk. He went to his desk and leaned back on his chair after everyone in the room turned silent. "Or maybe you come from the Italian section of Czechoslovakia or Austria, Senior DeAngelo?"

"You are from Italy, Mister DeAngelo," the old woman added. "More accurately, according to what some of us know, from a family in Sicily. Who were, and still are---"

"---Jews! Some of them, anyway. Mussolini made the trains run on time, but they took a whole lot of good people to bad places. Including...my family."

Vincent blasted out. "They were protectors of the poor who protected them from the rich, sometimes by going outside the law, which was owned by the rich, the fucking Church, and then by the Black Shirt goons who…" Vincent turned silent, recalling the horror stories Uncle Sal said happened to his other Uncles and grandparents, who decided to stay in the Old Country after El Duce took over. Vincent recalled the face of that tyrant. "Fascist bastard who----" he finally pushed out. Real tears came down Vincent's face, landing on quivering lips that were paralyzed by fear, anger, and guilt.

"Fascists, who did what?" he heard from Robert, the head Comrade laying his hand gently on Vincent's shaking shoulder.

"Probably the same thing that Hitler did to your people in the Old Country or are going to do very soon," Vincent self-observed himself pontificating and relating. "And what the Fascists will do to everyone everywhere if WE don't stop them! Freedom-loving stiffs who all have their different abilities, talents, and ways to fight dirty bastards as dirty as we have to. In ways we never did. And have to! No matter how many crooks who call themselves Presidents, Prime Ministers, and Police Commissioners try to stop us from doing what's right! And needed! Family is family, and we fight for all our families!"

The next sound was something Vincent had never heard after he had spoken his mind—applause, praise, and promotion to the head of the class and cavalry charge. It didn't matter that he held back some details about what some of his family business really was, not now, anyway. This was a war of common cause where everyone gets something out of it, even if they die trying. Or perhaps, especially if they die trying.

As for music to leave life stage left, Vincent heard the Internationale played on a violin by piano bar virtuoso by night Fred Gonzales, a fourth generation American whose brownish complexion still branded him a 'Mexican wetback'. Particularly when it came to getting promoted at any job, despite the fact that his vocabulary in English was far more extensive than most Gringos. Vinny recognized him on his 18th birthday when he was taken to the Flamingo Gentleman's Club by his Dad to consummate his new status as a man. And to be sure (by the report from the 'message' lady in the back room) that his son's 'more interested in connecting with women between the ears than between the legs' was due to his being some kind of classy gentleman rather than a perverted girly finocchio.

But the smile and understanding eyes on the 'win people's respect with music rather than a fist' Mexican-American Maestro were gone, as was his right hand. The stump extending from his twisted and charred elbow was strapped to a blood-stained bow. It extended his rage and lack of faith in the power of gentleness into every note (be they on tune or off) of the World Socialist Worker's Anthem he played on the fiddle.

"Another 'industrial accident' that the Capitalist bosses never reported at the Ford Plant in New Jersey," Robert explained regarding the Mexican's missing hand. "He lost his job the next day when it was discovered he was a Union organizer who wanted compensation for the others who had experienced 'accidents' on the job."

"Then couldn't get any other work anywhere else once the bosses got on the horn to each other in New York?" Vincent postulated.

"And Washington, to the democratically elected senators, congressmen, and President who want to stay on good terms with Henry Ford and his Capitalist cronies," Robert added. "Who is getting rich selling machinery and weapons to Hitler and Mussolini? Who is using Franco, the Church, and the Spanish fat cat aristocrats to destroy the democratically elected Republic in Spain? A Workers and Peasant's paradise where everyone gets what they need and gives back even more to everyone else. Maybe the first revolution in history where the transition from evil to goodness, oppression to freedom, widespread poverty to shared prosperity, that happened without collateral damage to the innocent, or even to the guilty, all things considered."

"But," Vincent countered respectfully, after putting his hand over his chin and assessing the bold claims about the new Camelot in Europe, according to his own knowledge and experience in 'God Blessed' America. "I read in the New York Times, Daily News, the Herald, and the Wall Street Journal----"

"---The lies that the shitheads in Washington and Wall Street want and need you to believe about the 'Socialist Communist Cancer'!" Robert informed the truth seeking but still not appropriately educated upstart. "Which Fritz Kuhn and his American Nazi Party right here say has to be stopped so THEY can make America pure and prosperous again? And which the 'good' and, truth be told, KKK-affiliated Catholic Pope-supported Father Coughlin preaches every Sunday on the radio to uneducated, vulnerable, and dangerously well-meaning apple pie and baseball-loving Americans. The lie that says everyone who is a Socialist or Communist is a Godless snake in the grass who will take away your hard-earned freedom," Robert, having exhausted his breath and patience, pulled his lips back, collecting his thoughts and integrating his mixed feelings. He released the new idea, incubating in his soul as it came to his always active mind after a smack of his tongue against his upper jaw. "Okay, We 'Anarchist Reds' should and WILL take away SOME freedoms from God-fearing

Kings, Capitalists, and Dictators, and those who want to be such. Like the freedom to rob, steal from, torture, or kill anyone less fortunate. The freedom to put the welfare of a selected few who you consider 'family' first, second, and last. With everyone else being…expendable. Worthless. Slaves whose life, liberty, the pursuit of happiness, a shot at a better life you steal from them. And, well…sometimes to do good things, we have to…" The scholar soldier for the Revolution eased his hand down towards his belt, laying it near the handle of a no-frills butcher's knife, bearing the inscription 'victory or death' in three languages as if it was a saber. "You know what I mean, don't you, Comrade DeAngelo?"

"Yeah, I do," Vincent replied, seeing from the corner of Robert's eyes that the battle lines had been drawn. That there was somewhere in all of this a clear distinction between Right and Wrong. And that not siding with what was Right did make you Wrong, both in the eyes of your Comrades and the inquisitor you had to encounter every time you really looked into a mirror.

CHAPTER 4

The road from Seneca Falls, New York, birthplace of the Women's Suffrage and (with the right kind of voting anyway) Equal Rights movement to the docks in lower Manhattan was long and hard. The main highway from Ithaca to Binghamton provided more potholes than flat surfaces for the 1927 Steward Dump Truck, which had been loaded up with privately donated medicines, food, clothing, and miscellaneous supplies required by the civilian army of Republicans in Spain to hold up against the onslaught of Generalissimo Franco and his Fascist Allies Beyond Binghamton. The latter included the 'the informed by somebody' Cops and US Army Reservists who set up roadblocks who were under orders to seize any goods and people headed for the Spanish 'Red rabble-rousers.'

Such forced the drivers of the truck to take backroads, which were more suited for horses than mechanized vehicles of any kind. Beyond Livingston, the truck decided to rebel against its drivers, perhaps because they had caused it much pain, injury, and 'discomfort.' Or maybe it was just old, and I decided it was time to retire to the junkyard. Such were its thoughts and hopes after the drivers, most probably bootleggers prior to the repeal of Prohibition by the size of their beer bellies and breath, who finally gave it a 'cool down' break in the middle of a dirt 'road' traversing a corn field. Though perhaps the break was more for the drivers, who took a beer, belch, and piss break under a full moon. But the beast made of metal and rubber decided not to obey its masters, refusing to take another step forward.

The loudest of the three four-legged creatures who had put the 6 going on 60 four-wheeled creatures through speeds, bumps, and jolts she was not built to take spoke up first. "Come on, you fucker!" Syracuse-born, raised, and conditioned Hershel Stein blasted at the engine when through his mouth while his foot pounded on the accelerator, his clenched cranking the key to the right so hard that it nearly broke in half. "We gave you ten minutes of rest, you bitch!" the washed up 'know it all' truck driver who boasted about his glory days as a defensive line football star at Syracuse University until his career was cut short by an offensive guard who hit him just as hard in the places he had illegally hit many others who had gotten in his way to get a 'gal winning' sac of the quarterback. "You're going to obey me, bitch!" he yelled at the truck, which taunted him with half starts. "We got a ship in Brooklyn waiting for these goods. And finally, a semi-legit real paycheck for delivery!"

"And cops on our tail who'll turn us into jailbirds again, and who will turn you into junk!" former bootlegger, gunrunner for the IRA, and present 'will do anything for a sandwich or a drink' forty-going-on-fifteen Sean O'Brien informed the vehicle as he opened the hood, placing his toolbelt next to the battery. "And yer gonna listen ta us, bitch! We're yer masters, now, Missy!"

"Or else it's curtains for you!" Hershel yelled back at the truck, doing his best to hide the fear he had if the 'miscellaneous' items in the truck were seen by the wrong Cop or Army Reservist.

Sean used whatever mechanical skills he had at the hood while Hershel tried to ram reason into the truck's 'head.' Then, as they called each other with a strange brand of respect, they didn't understand themselves, 'Kike' and 'Mick' did attempt to use some brains rather than brawn. But when the former failed to get 'Daisy' (the name of the truck given to it by the owner in Seneca Falls) moving again, their fear of being caught by the Cops or eaten by animals in the woods adjacent to the cornfield translated into all manner of insults delivered at Daisy. Such included bitch, cunt, and several others in each other's father's native tongue. Resolved to get the final word, Sean yanked out his hammer, Hershel his revolver. Both instruments were poised to destroy, or at least make a statement to, the mechanized source of their frustration.

From the woods emerged an intruder. Her entry startled both men, as they were used to mastering both machines and women. "Daisy will cooperate with you if you treat her with respect," the intruder noted in a haunting human and very feminine southern drawl, with Texan defiance embroiled around every vowel and confidence.

Sean and Hershel both turned themselves and their weapons on the intruder.

"A Steward dump truck," the young woman with straggly long blonde hair and old, tired eyes said as she looked at the truck. The intruder was clad in a white dress containing brown stains that looked and smelt like shit. "Daisy's givin' ya'll some trouble, I see, and have been hearin'?" she continued, as her cowboy boots, whose worn-out soles looked like they had been used for a long journey, made little or no imprint into the muddy ground en route to the engine. She laid her suitcase on the ground and then examined Daisy's 'innards.'

The moonlight flashing on her face revealed red bruises which were about to become black and blue. Her legs were shapely, sized perfectly, with tinges of blood just above the ankles, perhaps from walking too fast through the woods or not fast enough away from the wrong people. "Where ya'll headed?" she inquired as she inspected Daisy's mechanical 'soul,' more like movements of a delicate belle assessing a broken loom rather than a hard-working mechanic dealing with REAL machinery.

"We'd be goin' ta New York City," Sean boasted with his finest Irish borough, sticking out his chest with Gaelic pride. "And then---"

Hershel firmly placed the heel of his work boots on Sean's toes, silencing him as to their real destination once crossing over into City Limits. "And then, somewhere far from there…and here, Ma'am." He said with a courtly bow. "Just, maybe like you are?" he continued, pointing to her suitcase. "Miss…"

"Sally," she said. "Or Samantha, if you wanna call me that. Or anything else."

"What do ya get in that suitcase?" Sean challenged. "If you don't mind me askin'."

"Tools," the seemingly wayward farm maiden said, opening up the suitcase and grabbing what she needed, along with some rolls of tape. "Better ones than you have." She pointed to metal tools in her suitcase, which Sean or Hershel had never seen but which, somehow, made their contraband of 'implements for the fight against Fascism' in the truck look like surplus parts from the Spanish-American War back in 1898.

"And those?" Hershel said, pointing to books in another recess of the bag. Books that looked 'academic', some medical, some philosophical but most of them political.

"Tools for the head," 'Sally' said, after which she commenced to get Daisy back on her feet. "Which can be used to fix…well…maybe even her," she said regarding her mechanized 'patient.' "Any of you got a flashlight?"

"But yer a---" Hershel smirked.

"----Woman!" she pushed out with an angry grunt while bending over, seeing something deep inside Daisy's engine. "Yes, I guess I am; last time I checked in a mirror, that is," she went on as a submissive Southern belle. "With eyes in the back of my head as you gentlemen are looking upward between my legs," she continued, anticipating, correctly, the eyeline of the stranded 'going sort of straight for the right clients' affection and love-starved smugglers. "Which is fine with me. As long as ya look and don't touch."

Sean and Hershel felt like they were five years old, caught with their hand inside the cookie jar while another round of disallowed pastries were sticking out from their lips.

"So, I what yer problem is," Sally, or whoever she was, said. She pulled herself up from the truck, laying her feet on the ground with a hard and painful thump.

Sean and Hershel looked at each other, anticipating that Sally would perhaps give them answers as to why their lives turned out so wrong when they, according to what they thought anyway, were doing things so right. So, right, according to them anyway.

"The vacuum assist ta yer carburetor was disconnected," she said with a civil and respectful smile. "Which I'm reconnecting now." After completing the task with minimal action of her hands and more medical than mechanical tools, she proceeded with a limp to the driver's seat and started the vehicle.

Hershel and Sean were never more shocked. And relieved. And in need of thanking someone bigger than themselves. Particularly as they saw, over the horizon, what seemed to be one Army truck escorted by no less than three police cars turning towards their unintentional 'rest stop' in the farm field.

Hershel pulled out a fistful of money, offering it to the 'angel' sent by the wolves, the Fates, the Good Lord, or just Lady Luck. "For your trouble, Sally. A thank you," he said as he reached for the keys to the now started and good-sounding, for now anyway, truck.

"Which I won't accept," she stated firmly.

"Then will you accept this?" Sean said, removing his stash of gear from the back seat and placing his prized pillow on it for her comfort. "A free ride to---"

"---Peer 24 on at the Battery in Manhattan," she said, looking at the paperwork that had fallen on the floor from the glove compartment when Hershel was yelling at Daisy. "And…" she continued, eyeing the other paperwork scattered on the floor of the truck. "I'd be needin' a ride ta Spain as cargo. Por favor."

Sean and Hershel looked at each other, each one trying to blame the other for not hiding the documents as to their real destination. Each secretly hoped that their own guilt for being sloppy smugglers in their advancing age would not be detected by the other.

"And as for that cargo, if those boxes of Red Cross medical supplies and food in the back of the truck have inside of them some toxic bullets and guns to kill Fascist men, all the better," Sally continued, her accent strangely having traveled from Dixie to Upstate New York in a frightening millisecond.

Hershel planned on questioning 'Mick' Sean for sloppily packing the hidden guns anti-Fascist mobsters and well-meaning WWI veterans illegally packed in with the medical supplies, food, and food or for letting a wayward female stranger see them. Sean thought and felt the same about his Kike partner. But both men kept their inquires silent while Sally slid away from the comfort seat in the cab of the truck, and made her way to the cargo compartment. She buried herself as cargo under two thick blankets and a fake floorboard. "Andiamo, Comrades!" she yelled back to her escorts. Big men with big dreams in their youth who found themselves to be smaller men in their old age. Who would deliver their goods, collect their paycheck, dump off the mystery woman who miraculously had found them, then head back Upstate to the go-nowhere lives that at least allowed them to be somewhere…familiar.

CHAPTER 5

From under a slightly slanted beret, an oversized wool coat bearing several bullet holes, and behind a recently (and reluctantly) trimmed beard, Carlos Garcia bid a mixed collection of French gents, ladies, and dock inspects at Biarritz with 'have a great day' greetings en francais which he sensed matched their social expectations, hoping that his Spanish, or even more dangerously, Basque nationality would be not detected in his diction. And, more importantly, the contents of his hay-covered yet flounder-smelling horse-drawn wagon, which had just been loaded up with supplies for the Republican Cause at two beaches bearing no name by freelance 'just needed to get our boat patched up so we could get back home to the lassies after we hit a storm' Scottish fishermen would not be examined. Or even more importantly, he hoped that the passengers embarking from the swaying ladder precariously attached to the multi-storied tanker from the other side of the pond who Carlos was assigned to pick up, would know what to say and not say to the Customs and Immigration Officers. Those pristinely clad Guardians of France were taking more than the average amount of time to look for Socialist 'rabble-rousers' headed to join the Russian-backed Republican 'rebels' in Spain. Or, officially anyway, anyone who was on their way to lending a hand, gun, or suitcase of money to Franco and his Fascist Allies.

"I hope that this batch of Comrades has as much usefulness as enthusiasm," Carlos told the horse as he noted the first new recruit for the Cause. His brown hair with a bit of grey on the temples was neatly combed back on his clean-shaven, chiseled face. He sported a Chicago made brown vested business suit and Texan cowboy boots with real scuffs only made possible by many miles in the saddle. "At least this one is old enough to grow a real beard and probably knows more about cavalry chargers against the enemy than John Wayne, Buster Keaton, or Miguel Cervantes," Carlos related to the Belgian mare with feet as big as a Clydesdale and legs that could carry anything strapped on a wagon behind her as fast as any Thoroughbred could run without a rider. Such was, so far anyway, faster than most pursuit vehicles, as long as the chase wasn't on concrete.

"This volunteer is John Smith by name," Carlos related with rolling eyebrows to the mare upon hearing the American arrival state who he was to the first inspector. "Does he know that he's risking jail and deportation to another country other than his own if his real reason for being here is discovered before he gets to Republican-held Spain or winds up in Fascist-controlled areas?" he continued, recalling how this man who (according to the political and medical screeners in New York) refused to lie or be lied to. Those two skills, lying that is, were, of course, what one had to get used to in any War pitting man against man. Or, for that matter, domestic disputes between men and women.

"And the next one," Carlos continued to his grey equine Comrade, this time in Basque Spanish, as none of the gentrified Frenchmen or women around him were interested in his 'peasant working man's charm' anymore. "Tim Jackson," he said regarding the man who introduced himself to the Inspector as Leroy Jones. "A man of color, darker than either of us," the Basque handler said of the six-foot tall and ten feet proud Negro wearing an American Army tunic from the Great War bearing medals from the French Army for bravery in that conflict. Wrapping his muscular legs were torn, blood-stained trousers with leather footwear which were more rags than hides. "But, this Black veteran from a War fought for the rights and profits of White men has the Light of Hope, Justice, and what I hope isn't any more than a healthy dose of Revenge in his eyes," Carlos observed of the dark as coal, no doubt Grandson of a slave who stood in line behind John Smith. The white-as-toxic snow Aryan businessman who, if he was clad in a German Army uniform and trim around the ears, would be the poster Mensch for 'SS Fashion Model of the Year.'

Carlos looked into the eyes of the mare who had saved countless lives at the cost of shortening her own or, perhaps, making it longer due to its intense Purposefulness. He allowed himself to lose himself in her Soul, as was a necessity for reconciling himself as a Basque separatist and a loyal Republican Spaniard. He knew that freedom from the iron fist of Franco's Nationalists and their Fascist German and Italian backers would have to come before the Basques could declare their independence from Republican Spain. He dreamed of both events happening, smelling the food at both victory parades to happen within his lifetime, as well as the sweet aroma of flowers given to the Crusaders by grateful, liberated women and children, as well as if they wanted to expressively 'different' men.

Carlos was awakened from seeing, feeling and touching that dream work the dream world by the presence of a young man in a White Suit with Spats. By the way he disembarked the ship, he considered himself way too important to wait behind the long line of 'commoners,' many of which were shaking their legs so that they could hold in the urine inside their bladders on the slow-moving disembarking line. "Hey," he yelled at the Head Inspector, pulling out a wad of American greenbacks. "This in your pocket and for your crew if ya's let all of us get to our business with honest folks on shore while you and your crew get ta go home early. One hand washes the other, capiche?"

The Head Inspector halted the line, then addressed the dumb-as-nails 'Wiseguy.' "And your business for honest folks is what, Monsieur?" he blasted up to the 'smart in the head and smarter with contacts' Italian American who Carlos was told would be ideal for the intelligence branch of the Lincoln Brigade due to his underworld contacts and his knowledge of the language of Mussolini's heavily supplied army. "What is your business in France, Sir?" the Inspector asked with a bow that made him only appear to be socially inferior to Comrade Robert Stein's top recommendation as intelligence officer material in the International Brigade.

"I'm a...geologiere." Vincent DeAngelo replied, reading from something he had written on his arm as he rolled up his sleeve. "Ya know, a guy who studies rocks. Je suis un---"

"---Geologeire?" the Inspector, who had orders to stop anyone from entering France as a jumping board to 'stroll' on over to Spain, enquired with a mocking grin. He instructed his men to take the Wiseguy and promote him to the front of the line.

The port inspectors edged their way towards Vincent, who froze in place. The New York Wiseguy seemed to be caught between bashing his back against a steel wall, running the gauntlet to the left, scurrying to the right, or jumping down into the cold harbor water. But before he could make his decision, Vincent's left arm was held firmly by another hand from behind.

"He means a geologist, a well-meaning young genius who knows rocks and hiding places for oil can be drilled more than he knows people," a blonde babe who looked like she just stepped off a Hollywood film set, in full makeup, said to the Head Inspector, in what Carlos recognized as a different kind of French. "My name is Sally. Sally DeBois. And my husband's knowledge of French is not quite up to what it should be," she continued en francais, gracefully inserting her slender, elegantly clad arm under Vincent's shaking, muscular elbow. "Isn't that right, Doctor Johnson?"

Vincent nodded in a professorial manner. "Oui," he said to the best of his linguistic ability.

The junior inspectors, whose eyes were held hostage by the woman's charm and gentle intelligence behind it, seemed satisfied. But the Head Inspector wasn't.

"Oui," you say, Doctor Johnson?" he mused, staring at and into Vincent, who somehow held on to a poker face that was getting thinner by the second. "And you, Mademoiselle. Your French sounds like YOU are from…"

"…Quebec," Vincent replied in English. "Where me and my wife met," he said of the babe who picked him up before he was about to be picked out for deportation back home to the US or importation to a French jail cell. "And promised ourselves years ago that we'd be married here, in the country where REAL love was invented."

"And where learned how to bastardize the language of your French men and women ancestors," the Inspector said through a chuckle. "But I will need to see your papers."

With a flick of his fingers from his position at the peer, he requested the happy couple to come forth. He halted them, and insisted on each one handing him their papers, starting with Vincent.

"Say something in geologiere, Sir," the Inspector requested.

Vincent thought a moment, then just in the nick of time, related something in Latin which sounded scientific, to Carlos anyway. And apparently to the Inspector as well.

"And that means?" the Customs Agent asked 'the professor's' wife.

"That he and we can find out where there is oil in this country and make sure that France gets to keep it," Sally replied.

"Or sell it to whoever you want, for whatever you want," Professor Vincent added.

The Inspector glanced at their papers, the best that Russian forgers in New York could provide, Carlos recalled. And hope was still true. After two real looks at the papers and one added just to make him look official, the Inspector returned the document and then inserted a card into Vincent's pocket.

"My brother is a priest, and my cousin owns a resort that is perfect for your honeymoon. And my son operates a company that, well, may want to do business with you, for the good of France, of course," the Inspector related with a smile. "And I expect an invitation, of course."

"Of course," Sally said in French. "It would be a pleasure."

"No problem!" Vincent replied in New Yawkese.

The Inspector motioned the happy couple on, then, with a welcoming smile, proceeded personally with the interrogation of the next foreign arrival to his beloved country. His men, who usually searched every tenth bag or suitcase, opened each one, examining the contents with their eyes and fingers.

"Right, no problem!" Carlos slurred out of his mouth, in his native Basque, to his mare, who was enough of a stallion at heart to deserve the name of 'Cervantes.' After which, he drove the wagon to the Inn where this round of American tourists was to check in for a briefing, a homecooked French meal, a change of attire, and, as was probably to be required, a departure out the back door before the sun rose.

CHAPTER 6

"It wasn't Mother Nature's idea to push out of the Pyrenees Mountains between Spain and France, but perhaps she had her reasons," Carlos related to the four Yanks at a clearing in the woods not visible to their hotel where Carlos had set up a late supper 'picnic.' By complete accident, Life had assigned to him to escort them to their new liberated lives, or perhaps early glorious deaths, as fighters for Democracy as new members of the Abraham Lincoln Brigade in Spain. "In 711 A.D., the Moors brought Islam, Literacy, and Learning to the barbarian Christians of Spain," he went on to the Americans as they beheld the tall snow-covered peaks from the foothills while the sunset in the West. "But for whatever reason, Mother Nature didn't want them to offer their different and more Enlightened perspectives to France, sparing the illiterate French from the agonies that happen when you start to read. And the mountains allowed Islamic, Jewish, and Christian Scholars in Moorish Spain to develop their minds rather than to have to become better soldiers to protect the libraries from being overrun by French

Christians," he continued from his blacked face as the first stars appeared in the blacking sky from the hills overlooking the moonlit border crossing below, which now had three times more guards than a week before with twice as many weapons, their assigned job being to turn away everyone seeking entry to Spain.

"But there is a Basque saying that if you listen to what the mountains are telling you, they will let you go through them safely and with gifts to your heart and mind, you will understand when you reach the other side," Carlos assured the band of four whose feet were already shivering in the deep snow, and Cervantes, whose hooves he had equipped with grips for the underlying ice. "And another thing the mountain reminds us about is that societies who invented the wheel are not always the ones that are most advanced," he revealed with a smile as he adjusted the makeshift sleds harnessed to the horse and backpacks on the backs of him and his fellow humans containing guns, ammo, medicines and food he had off-loaded from the wagon. "And there is a Spanish motto from the days of El Cid that said----"

"---It's too fucking cold for a moonlight stroll across a mountain range," Vincent protested through quivering lips, his torso covered with more coats, sweaters, and scarves than any of his Comrades and shivering three times more intensely.

"But a man's gotta do what a man's gotta do," Tim Jackson interjected with a firm nod as he harnessed himself to one of the contraband-loaded sleds.

"And a woman, too," Sally insisted, strapping herself as a draft horse to the heaviest the sleds.

"Indeed, yes," John Smith added as he took on his share of the loads to be transported, then glanced at the white-capped mountains ahead of him. "High mountains they are," he noted, apprehension behind his stoic face. A Midwesterner who had been born, raised, and conditioned to flat land where a hill four stories high was considered a mountain. "Yeah…very---"

"---Scary, but only if you look down," Carlos assured him. "But if you want, and need, to turn back, there is no disgrace to it," he said to Smith, laying his assuring blistered and injured more times than he could remember hand on his shoulder. "Or," he continued, looking into the darkening faces of the others. "If any of the rest of you want to or need to turn back, we and the Democratic Revolution will understand."

"But our ancestors won't," Sally affirmed. With even deeper secrets behind her determined eyes, she headed down the snowy hill, using only her compass as the way to negotiate the path ahead, tossing the map provided for her into the snow.

"Neither will the women who are watching us, or we wanna return to one day won't understand us doing the safe instead of the heroic thing," Tim said, following Sally.

"Or our families," Smith realized and related, shoving off towards the caravan, courage somehow infiltrating into him.

Or THE Family," Vincent concluded. "May as well make it a quartet," he went on, hiding his terrified face from Carlos and the urine stain that had established itself between his legs.

Carlos turned to Cervantes. "And a quintet or sextet?" he inquired of the supply-loaded mare, who froze in place, her legs locking into rigid extensions. "Just one more time," he assured the mare who had previously obeyed every command and request he had presented to her. But despite his trying to draw her attention to him, the mare's ears oscillated back and forth, sensing danger to the right, left, and behind her. Her feet pounded on the snow as if trying to say something.

Indeed, Carlos felt he was being watched also, and not only by wolves looking for an easy meal of horse and human meat during a winter when, at least in Republican-held Spain, there was a paucity of food for man and beast. But he did know one thing. "Hey!" he said, looking straight into Cervantes' large and watchful left eye, holding it in place with a determined stare. "Forward is the only direction we, and you, have left. The only way to not get devoured by the ghosts of our imaginations or the cowardly demons of our past, Comprende?"

Stroking his already frosted and ice-covered beard, Carlos allowed himself to think that the horse answered 'yes.' It was another belief that was a lie, perhaps, but one that could be converted into a Truth with enough determination and, of course, luck. And, of course, there was the advice of the Pyrenees mountains, whose peaks seemed to speak to Carlos in that language of loud Silence that he always felt but was not allowed to understand. Accepting their invitation or challenge, Carlos took the first step Southward, nearly slipping on the ice but somehow pulling himself back upright with brains in his feet that he had learned to trust far more than any smarts in his head.

"Well, are you coming or not?" Sally yelled out to the others in the caravan. Tim Jackson was the first to follow her, after which John Smith began his sojourn. Due to his fear of being left behind or having to go home to a disappointed father and uncle, Vincent pushed his shivering body forward.

It was an even more challenging series of steep 'ups' and slippery 'downs' than Carlos could recall in any of the 'routine moonlight strolls' he had invited new recruits for the Cause to take. The 'brains in the guts' of mountaineer-raised Basque were keener than ever as he guided the foursome of Comrades forward. Surprisingly, with each step, these idealistic American heroes and/or fools found grounding within themselves and even with the Soul of the Mountains, which seemed to become their friends. They felt less alone, progressively immune from the contagious disease of fear. Not so for Carlos, whose mountaineer Basque roots made him more fearful and vulnerable with each step on this particular trip.

"Leave us alone, and we will leave you alone, Basajuan!" Carlos calmly yelled back to the intruder he felt and saw through the corner of his eye, with each turn in the path delineated by blue markers on the still-standing trees. "Go back to your cave, and I promise I or my companions won't tell anyone that you and your families still live here," he promised the, as he saw it anyway, hairy sharp-clawed Wildman of the woods (aka 'Bigfoot' to the Americans) who had been intrinsic to Basque religion before they were the last to convert to Christianity in the 12the Century. A man-beast who remained in their folklore and secretly believed hybrid religion.

But despite Carlos' pleading, warning, and trying to evade Basajuan and most probably members of his family, the intruder continued to follow, flanking the party on both sides. Carlos' partially snow-blind eyes saw tracks that looked like they could have been beloved, feared, and (to trespassers on their land, according to legend) vicious man-beast who could understand human language but dared not speak it. "If you want to take part in this War to preserve Democracy," Carlos proposed to the felt but not clearly seen hairy giants in his own language. "We can give you, as we did to women, the right to vote. But I'll have to propose it to the appropriate parties. After all, we Democratic Socialists are not anarchists."

"What's he saying, Sally?" Carlos heard from Tim, the only male multilingual member of the party, from directly behind him.

"And who the fuck is he talking to?" Vinny inquired through less huffing and puffing than he was experiencing in the first three miles of the 'stroll.'

"And in what language?" height-scared flatlander and now, hopefully anyway, adventurous mountaineer 'John Smith' (if indeed that was his real name) inquired of the young woman who always spoke last, with authority, and revealing only a small portion of what she was really thinking.

"I don't know," Sally replied after a long pause. "But something that's keeping the ghosts from gobbling us up and the wolves from eating us, Right Comrades?"

Tim replied with a 'right Comrade' to her, as did Vinny. Smith's response lacked that form of address that all Party members and Union men in the

Movement used. Such was not surprising to Carlos, as Smith was one of those rare American Socialists who had proudly not become a member of any political party or Worker's organization until he knew the real agenda of those groups and the innermost goals of their leaders. Something that, of course, no one could ever know for certain.

The sojourn of tired feet, frozen hands, and tested souls ended as the rising sun replaced the moon, placing the party two hundred yards south of the southern side of one of the stone cairns marking the Spanish border.

Carlos, after sending his accomplished and (to themselves as well as to him) unexpectedly courageous foursome down the hill towards the warmer slopes leading to the somewhat warmer Spanish valleys, looked behind him. Basajuan and his family, or perhaps a 'crew' of 'no trespassers allowed' enforcers, seemed to be watching him. He boldly approached the perhaps real, this time head 'shadow' behind the trees. He discreetly reached for his Soviet-made 20-year-old rifle with his hidden left hand and with his right threw towards the creature still lingering in the brush a package of dried pork and baguettes. He intended to provide his Comrades with a 'well done' breakfast toward it.

"The meat is maybe too spicy for your taste, and the pastry a bit too 'French,' but… an offering. Tribute.

As we move along back to our fellow, more primitive less hairy human brothers and sisters. Okay?" he asked the being behind the shadow, which seemed to change shape into ten different animals, as Aatxe, the shapeshifter, was known to do. Then, into Akerbeltz, the demon who appears as a goat. Who perhaps could be shot and killed for good by bullets provided by the Soviet Union, that country being a new experiment in the history of the world whose mandate was to believe in humanity rather than any kind of angels, demons, or Deity invented by Capitalist Priests to keep their power over ignorant masses.

The elusive yet ever-present visitor leaned down into the snow, the dark woods hiding its form and purpose. It picked up the package of culinary delights. The beast smelled it, then tasted it, then put something inside of it, then…tossed it back to Carlos, landing it in front of his feet.

Carlos opened the package, finding inside of it a piece of paper. "I and we can't be bought off that easily. We will meet again," he read in English. Fearing that the realm you can touch is far more dangerous than the one you can feel, the Basque Socialist aimed his rifle at the intruder. "Who are you?!" he demanded to know.

Jovial laughter came from the figure behind the shadowed brush. Light from the soon-to-be-rising sun cast light on the beast hiding in the woods. It was clearly a man or woman whose arms and legs were not covered with a big, thick coat of body hair.

"Who are you?!" Carlos demanded yet again of the intruder, who he had, perhaps, imagined as being from another realm. Or perhaps not. "Who are you!" he demanded in English, then German, then Italian, then Spanish, then French, then finally Basque as he walked with increasing fear-fed determination towards the apparently hungry for something other than a late night snack stalker.

The laughter from the bush continued, becoming more mocking and condescending with each step he took. "Who are you!" Carlos demanded, finally, in English, to the very real visitor to his mountains who stood his ground, even after four warning shots the Basque had fired at his, or her, feet.

Another note was thrown out to Carlos, attached to a rock. He opened it up, gazing pensively at its contents. "Ask the comrades you just liberated who I am," it read in very even red ink, or perhaps blood. "Then ask yourself. We have unfinished business."

"What business!" Carlos blasted out, looking up toward the deliverer of the note. Who, in the three seconds the smartest Basque in the Republican Army turned his back from, had disappeared. To be replaced by…nothing. With no comment as to what had just happened from Astxi, Akerbelts or Basajuan. Only voiceless quiet from the mountains spoke to Carlos in this hour of most need and deepest inquiry. He got even less from his horse, Cervantes, named after the author whose novel Don Quixote championed idealistic dreams over meat and potatoes reality. The reality, the sadistic yet sustaining beast that it was, had hit hard. It was made harder somehow by hearing Comrade Sally, Comrade Tim, Comrade John, and Comrade Vinny singing the Internationale from the valle, joined in by optimistic voices of other Republican Freedom Fighters who had greeted them.

Cervantes turned to Carlos, nudging his shaking shoulder with her head. Did she want food, anticipating oats instead of scrub grass under the snow for her breakfast? Or did she know something Carlos was slow to learn, and had to learn quickly. In any case, he moved 'forward' to his fellow real-world Republicans and the most reliably moralistic Cause available.

CHAPTER 7

"The very same bourgeois mentality which extols the manufacturing division of labour, the life-long annexation of the worker to a partial operation, and the unconditional subordination of the detail worker to capital, extols them as an organization of labour which increases productivity - denounces just as loudly every kind of deliberate social control and regulation of the social process of production, denounces it as an invasion of the inviolable property rights, liberty and self-determining genius of the individual capitalist," the 'Morale Officer' proclaimed loudly declared to the collection of civilian volunteers who had to be turned into soldiers to defend the Republican Democracy, reading from Das Capital with the focus and enthusiasm of a Baptist Preacher from what had been a pristine village square prior to its being stripped of most of its intact buildings and all of its people.

"He coulda just said, 'each should give according to their ability and take according to his needs,'" Tim

Jackson whispered to the partially newly uniformed man next to him while standing at less than rigid 'attention.'

"Or it's better ta be part of the fucking solution instead of a pain in the ass problem," 'Comrade Private' Vinny slurred out of his recently well-feed mouth. "Workin' for the good of others instead of just yourself."

"And, in your own way, working for the glory of God, who is an essential ingredient of this people's revolution for all humanity," Smith added, after which the Moral Officer went on about how religion is the toxic opioid of the masses. "Lenin's Revolution in Russia would have been a lot more effective if when he threw out religion he kept Spirituality."

"Without separation of Church and State, the priests ordained by the infallible Pope have more power than democratically, or sort a democratically elected Presidents," Tim offered.

"Priests who never go to bed hungry, and who secretly take to their bed a whole lot of kids who…." Vinny related, the rest of his rant halted by memories in his past which emerged into consciousness, yet again. After which he took in a deep breath, allowing the fire to come out of his mouth rather than burn a deeper hole in his conflicted and hurting soul. "Kids who WILL, someday, get payback from those fucks.

And the Nuns who…fucked up girls, and boys who---
"

"---Will become effective men, for the Cause of separating Church and State, and fighting Fascism, if you listen to the Comrade Captain up there, Comrade Private," he heard from an officer behind him.

Vinny silenced his mouth, but not his soul, as the well-meaning but poorly understood Spanish Morale Officer bearing the Red Star on his cap and handless stump doubling as his left arm continued the sermon. Finally, the pontification of Socialist ideals, which opposed any Papal rule, ended.

"I proudly salute you all for joining our Cause!" he finally proclaimed, with enormous pride, clenching his right hand in a fist and raising it against his ear. "Our Salute which we all give to each other!"

"When in Rome," Tim noted with resignation, placing his fist onto his 32 years of experience temple, along with the other recruits around him. Most of them were a decade or more younger than him. They were enthusiastically playing 'soldier' with the snap in their salute which belied the fact that they had never been in a war. Or perhaps even a street fight.

"Some fabricated gestures of requests do become necessary to maintain respect," Smith acknowledged, snapping to attention while doing the Republican Liberation Army salute he had seen in the newspapers but didn't believe was actually done. "So, are you in or out?" he asked Vinny, whose right hand clenched a fist but had not been raised to his defiant head, the only hold out in the, to his mind anyway, civilian volunteer army.

"Suppose it goes with this gay beret they asked us to wear," Vincent conceded with a whisper. "Long live the Republic, fellow Comrades!" he yelled out with a show of pride and hyper military demeanor and a more enthusiastic salute than anyone on the dusty parade ground, including the Morale Officer. "We're all in this together! Liberty or Death!"

Vincent's conversion from doubtful civilian to enthusiastic soldier inspired those around him as each of his declarations of freedom, all improvised, were repeated by everyone around him. Including, eventually, Tim and Smith. And finally, the Moral Officer.

All of this was witnessed and absorbed by Sally, watching on from the entrance of the abandoned, then looted general store, now converted into Field Hospital. It was as overloaded with patients as it was understocked with supplies. Such included French, Italian, German, Polish and a few English soldiers who had joined the International Brigades. They were, for the most part, older than the American volunteers. With a lot more experience as soldiers. And even more importantly for many of them, their experience as captives who had learned to fight their way out of concentration camps that officially did not exist, either in the newspapers of their native country or in any published articles in established publications printed in the so called 'free world'.

The rest of the cots, elevated boards, and straw-covered floor space were occupied by an even larger population of injured Spanish civilians who had somehow survived the invasion by Franco's Nationalist soldiers. There were also a fair number of as well as civilians who taken it upon themselves to rid Iberia of 'the Communist cancer'. Some decided to join the Socialist Republican Cause, some were, so they said, considering it.

Medical supplies were scarce. But not so the boys and girls who would never again be able to experience childhood. And women whose heads had been shaved and vaginas violated by the well-paid, well-fed, and tastefully clad Fascist soldiers after their husbands and brothers had been killed, or worse.

"And now," Sally heard from a broad-chested and baritone-voiced Herclean Captain whose mismatched military attire under his medical lab coat and Fu Manchu mustache made him seem more accomplished than his rank. "The training for these men begins," Comrade Doctor Juan Fernandez, a multi-scar bearing yet somehow still-alive thirty-year-old soldier who had experienced more combat in the last year than his father and grandfather had endured in a lifetime, said to Sally regarding her three male American compadres and the other Yankee volunteers on the parade ground.

"And for the women?" Sally inquired, referring to both herself and three other vagina-bearing volunteers behind her who had been 'excused' from boot camp training.

"What about real guns?" Sally commented, pointing to the broomsticks to be distributed to the collection of mostly civilians whose knowledge of real warfare was restricted to war movies and tall tales from their fathers or older brothers.

"They'll get them soon enough," the Comrade Doctor Captain assured. "Very soon. Too soon," he continued with a downward turned head and averted blank stare.

"A day after they learn how to charge a hill with pitchforks, they get a rifle, a hundred bullets, and a 'we wish you well' Comrade salute?'" she surmised and stated, giving the officer in the army she was disallowed to officially join the 'fraternity' salute.

"And you can do better than that?" Fernandez challenged.

Demonstrating her point, Sally grabbed hold of his Soviet rifle with her left hand and tossed into the air three nearly empty bottles of rum with her right. With alacrity and pleasure, she dispersed them into broken glass before they hit the ground. Then, as Fernandez and the rest of the men in camp gazed with shock, she whipped out the good Captain's knife, wrestling him to the ground in a swift action, mockingly slitting his throat. "And as for any other man who thinks he is stronger than any woman," she continued, inviting three heavily armed with muscle and weaponry to have at her. After they accepted the challenge, she nailed them into the dirt, relieving them of their guns, knives, and the manhood between their shaking and, in one case, urine-stained legs. The women delegated to be nurses, cooks, or perhaps service providers for a man's carnal needs behind Sally smirked with vicarious satisfaction.

"And I can fix anything made of metal and or flesh that gets torn apart, as good as any man here!" Sally boasted, after which she turned to her new 'sisters.' "Right, Comrade sisters?"

Indeed, yes, Fernandez said to Sally. "Comrade Doctor Sally…"

"Williamson," she replied with a proud truth-withholding grin. "Or Gonzales. Or Kewlaski. Or Kewalskov. Or any other name that looks good for the recruiting poster, the newspapers… Or my tombstone, eventually."

Reflective Silence took over the camp. Each soul who was there by choice or circumstance reflected his or her own relationship with birth, death, and the experience called life in between. It was finally broken by a one-armed child who played a song on the harmonica which Sally didn't recognize, and She said 'thank you for being here' to her with his eyes. His solo performance was joined in with instruments ranging from spoons to fiddles. And then by the voice from anyone whose tongue could hum along or improvise lyrics to in their own language.

Sally allowed herself to become lost in the young boy's brown-blue ocular portholes, imagining what her life would have been if she had elected to buy into motherhood. And thinking that evolved into dreaming about indulging in that most basic and needed institution with the right man. The optimal candidate for such came into her sight.

As Captain Fernandez looked at and into Sally's soul, he seemed to have intensity of soul, kindness of heart, and (with some education regarding women's rights) intelligence of mind. The kind of Comrade who could appreciate her as someone who, from the earliest she could remember, went through life because she had to rather than because she wanted to. It was a trait that perhaps made her the genius she had (without permission from any man) become. Something the mostly self-taught 'whiz at most everything' would lose, of course, if she allowed herself to want anything, particularly a man such as Comrade Captain, former professor, and current overly diplomate-d Doctor Fernandez.

CHAPTER 8

After being taught by an intense woman battling herself every day as to what to do to enemy men in combat, the current group of Abraham Lincoln Brigade recruits was sent out to apply their newly learned skills. They were armed with rifles ten or more years older than the weapons provided by the German and Italian Fascists to Franco's soldiers. They each received a hundred rounds of ammunition and a rousing send-off from women and children who really DID believe that they all would come back to be husbands and step-fathers to somebody someday soon. Each was assigned a different position in an army where everyone was considered equal with regard to the soul but with recognized inequalities in skills, mental and physical. And as well with regard to their potential leadership abilities. They were sent to battle in small groups through different routes so the Italian Fiat Cr 32 and German Ju 50 planes would not spot them.

"It's proper and right that you're settin' on that horse, leading us to battle, Comrade Squad Leader," Tim Jackson noted from his position as an infantryman to the mounted leader of the 12 men in his 'group,' most but not all of them non-Spaniards.

"All I did was tell them I could ride a horse," John Smith related with humility.

"Which you do better than any other man in this platoon," Jackson reminded Smith. "Someone's got to ride the few horses we still got. Which we can use to pull artillery, ride through the woods to do quick, unnoticed reconnaissance on the Fascists, get messages ta other platoons and headquarters faster and quieter than any truck or motorbike and, besides---"

"----someone's got to look and talk like a grandpa Cavalry officer who knows where the Injuns and Fascist banditos are," Infantryman, by way of example, and temporary Morale Officer Vincent DeAngelo offered sarcastically. "Who's officially a Corporal, A Corporal who doesn't know where the goddamn Fascists are. Or their Irish, Portuguese, and, if you'll excuse the fucking expression, Moroccan Nigger mercenaries are."

"But I can smell where they are," Jackson reminded DeAngelo, out of ear range from the other Brigade Members, whose complexion was many shades lighter than his own. "Then I whisper what we should do to Comrade Lieutenant Smith, here. Cause most of these wannabe Commie crackers around us won't listen to a Black man."

"And when Comrade Commander Smith tries to talk the Fascists into laying down their machine guns and pounding their bayonets into fucking plowshares," Vincent spat into Jackson's face.

"It's plowshares, not plowshares," midWestern farm belt raised Smith sneered back at DeAngelo, having had enough threats and 'any place other than New York is hoaky as shit' insults from the clever and potentially vicious mobster in training. With the eyes in the back of his now lice-infested head, Smith took a gander at the 'lads' behind him, who were as wet behind the ears as he was. Each one of them had been bucked off the proud cut gelding Smith was able to reach an agreement with. They all would give their left and right testicles for a shower, better-fitting boots, and a hot meal, or for that matter, any meal that would really fill the stomach. "We are all in this together, right!" Smith proclaimed as the leader his father had been in the Great War, or so his father claimed he was anyway in his letters. Correspondences infused with expressions of love and glory, which stopped abruptly a month before the Armistice of November 1918. The last indication is about or from the man who went to War so his sons would not have to.

John Smith thought about the other son his father spawned. His brother Orville was a jailbird who, prior to his incarceration for extortion, bank robbery, and murder, was the heroic carrier of the family name. John heard the guns in the distance. He assured his horse and the men under his command that they would be silenced very soon, then sank back into memories about Orville. He recalled memories of his more colorful, popular, and likable brother before he got caught and sent to the Big House. How John envied his smarter, stronger, and lovable brother, whose face he saw every time he looked at his daughter's face following her fourth birthday. Yes, Orville was a man who was not cursed with a conscience.

"But then again, a brother or a sister is the person whose soul you least know and prevent yourself from really finding out about," John Smith pondered as he recalled the good days with Orville when growing up on the family farm and soon afterward in town. Days that perhaps weren't so good. But days in the past, you kept trying to re-create in the present, at least according to your best imagination of them. 'Johnboy' Smith pondered yet again if he, as the 'virtuous and kind' son, was a disappointment rather than a source of pride to his very American father. An All-American Dad who embraced competition, honoring the winner of every 'game,' no matter how the victory was obtained. "I wonder what Orville and Pa would think of me now," he asked the proud-cut jet-black gelding who carried himself off as a stallion. "Or what your father thinks of YOU now, which is---"

The Andalusian-Arab steed between Smith's legs turned his ears to the moving branches in the thicket of windless woods to his left, then snapped his head to them. The (at least for Smith) usually obedient steed snorted, preparing to rush at, rather than away, from the unexpected intruder or intruders. With one hand holding the determined steed's head down and another on his rifle, Smith prepared to meet the enemy. The infantrymen beside him crouched down, aiming the business end of their mostly outdated firearms at the commotion. "Who goes there? Identify yourself!" Smith demanded, in his best Spanish.

"A friend," Smith heard from a familiar voice, the rider atop a mare who was more interested in getting to know Smith's horse than developing a deeper understanding of her own rider, provider, and best friend. Carlos, proudly atop Cervantes, respectfully corrected Smith's Spanish grammar and diction, including adding the 'lisp' that Americans, mostly 'red-blooded' American men, neglected to insert into Spanish for fear of being mistaken as 'less than manly.' Then Carlos asked where Smith and his new Comrades were going.

"To defend Jarama!" Vincent blurted out proudly.

The Republican Spaniards, who Vincent considered under his command repeated the town's name, replacing the J sound with a W.

"Where I heard there are a lot of olive trees," Vincent recalled from his youth as an overfed stock boy assigned by his Sicilian Uncle to keep an eye on their Greek food importing partners in Brooklyn, to the accompaniment of growling from his empty stomach, and everyone else's in the present food-challenged times of the Great Depression. "Best olives south of the North Pole. And the biggest! A small palmful of them is a full meal for anyone's hungry belly! Better than any field mouse, wild pig butt, or squirrel leg bread balls. Or dead Nationalist Fascist ribeye."

"Which I didn't put into the stew, last time anyway," Tim Jackson, the company's head cook by CHOICE, added. "White Fascist human meat doesn't have much taste anyway. And way too much fat."

A communal laugh took over the platoon. It was amplified by more morale-boosting comments regarding how one can and had to pretend that two bites of an onion, four beans, and a small thin slice of stale bread under the cold Spanish sky could make the brain feel it was a Thanksgiving feast under the roof of a warm, family dinner at home. But there was one 'diner' at the fabricated table whose absence concerned Carlos most.

"Where's Comrade Sally?" Carlos inquired of Smith, pulling him away from the 'festival.'

"Training new men to be more effective soldiers, soldiers, I assume," his reply. "Teaching more women to be less dependent on men," the oldest and perhaps more inwardly experienced member of the platoon went on, with as much pity as privately felt animosity. "And," he continued, graciously acknowledging his relational limitations. "Showing off her skills as a doctor to the Spanish physician who keeps reminding her to spend SOME time healing herself with him." Smith's face seemed to start dreaming again about who to take home or who to remain away from home with. "Why do you ask?" Smith inquired of Carlos.

"She'll be more useful to us here than anyone else back there," Carlos replied, looking behind him.

"As a fighter, teacher, or doctor?" Smith asked.

"All of the above," the sombre reply.

"And…maybe a woman who's watching all of us men. Who will inspire all of us, men, to compete to be the bravest hero who she will reward with, well,…." Smith continued, searching for the right descriptor.

"Her smile?" Carlos interjected.

"Yes," Smith concluded, his chapped lips breaking into a professorial grin of acceptance and internal accomplishment, somehow.

The short-term pleasure was interrupted by a barrage of bullets from an over-flying plane. It sprayed lead into trees, dirt, and rocks rather than human or equine flesh this time. There was a thin layer of frost on the ground, which smelled of urine after the platoon got back up on its tired feet.

"Andiomo, muchachos!" Smith self-observed himself, declared from atop his horse, leading the platoon onward. A group of dedicated misfits armed with its Winchesters, Gewher, and Manhlicker rifles manufactured fifty years ago, against the Italian and German-made small arms and artillery produced in the last 10 years by highly paid engineers.

Carlos watched on, knowing that there were four types of men who emerged after their first 10 seconds of real-life combat or any time afterward. Those who do what they have to with clear-thinking minds and controlled, or deadened, emotions. Those who run away from danger when presented with it. Those who turn catatonic, shell-shocked victims who are easy prey for being killed or captured by the enemy or shot by their own superiors. Or, more effectively and tragically, those who find that they enjoy killing, sprouting a third leg in their groin when taking the life of any enemy combatant and, soon afterward, anyone else. Who would be what? Carlos, a veteran of innumerable battles already, didn't know, especially about himself.

CHAPTER 9

Mother Nature felt that it was time to get rid of her most cerebrally advanced, well-fed, and least grateful species, as she decided to send winter rains on both sides of the river in Jamara in January, which led to hard ground the next month. Such disabled either side to dig trenches or fox holes. "This means that something bigger than us is heralding a quick victory instead of a prolonged war where we hide in trenches for months at a time and die of boredom, starvation, and trench foot," the Generals on both sides told their troops. The Nationalists troops under Franco, who was under Hitler and Mussolini, claimed that Mother Nature was in service of God. The Republican high command, in league with and in need of the Soviets, explained that the 'something bigger than us' was based on 'the biology of Nature and the natural rise of the proletariat.'

By the time the Abraham Lincoln Brigade reached Jamara two weeks after Franco's troops invaded it, the green valley had been converted into a treeless expanse of charred earth with trenches constructed of broken stone walls, salvaged wood from blown up homes, rocks uncovered from the limestone earth and, when they ran out of those, equine, bovine and human corpses. Everyone and everything that wasn't wearing a uniform had fled. The aroma of early spring grass was replaced by the stench of death.

"So, tell me why we're defending this valley that doesn't have any people, animals, or olives left in it," Smith asked Carlos upon arrival, voicing the sentiments of everyone under his command. All of the men were having second thoughts about the legal options entailed with being a 'volunteer' with citizenships in a foreign country that did not take any official loyalty oath.

"If the Fascists take this valley, they'll cut off the still free people and Worker's Army in Madrid from Valencia, which will cut us off from all the territories we recaptured in the last six months after nearly being wiped out in Madrid," Carlos explained after taking in a deep breath, looking at and into every member of the Platoon, most of whom had never been shot, nor shot anyone else.

"And what about those people over there?" Vincent inquired, noting Republican unarmed troops across the valley being escorted at gunpoint by armed and angry Republicans on a path leading up to a mountain cave behind him.

"Mutineers, maybe?" Tim suggested, recalling his time in the trenches when front-line French conscripts decided that their own lives were more important than the orders given to them by backline generals.

Before Carlos could confess a positive answer to that question, Tim intervened. "Or maybe they're conscience-less Fascists who tried to infiltrate our lines by posing as freedom-fighting Republicans and were caught."

"Not like the Moroccan mercenaries who got into our British volunteers' trenches because they sang the Internationale, then turned their guns on our brave and believing lads and took them all prisoner last week," Carlos related as he surrendered his horse to an underaged lad to bring to the safety, instructing Smith to do the same. "Prisoners who will…yes, wish they would have been killed. Who won't see home again."

"We can pretend to liberate' them!" Vincent asserted, grabbing hold of an 1895 Browning Colt machine gun from a three-legged wheeled wagon behind him. "I can pass myself off as an Italian who can infiltrate the prison or concentration camp. Lead any one of you who wants to follow me and get them all out. Where are they?"

"On the other side of that hill," Carlos explained, pointing to the steep incline on the opposite side of the valley covered with lines of Nationalist troops armed with bigger and more shiny than their own. The weapons and troops were being blessed by Catholic Priests in black cossacks and white collars, some with guns and scalps strapped to their waists. "A hill which---"

"---we've been ordered to take," came from a voice behind the recently arrived platoon. The emitter of that declared affirmation was from no other than Colonel Robert Hale Merriman, the commanding officer of the, reportedly anyway, nearly 2,000 going on 3,000 Americans in the Abraham Lincoln and Washington Brigades. It was none other than the tall, muscular ex-Sargent in the US Army who, as a Comrade General, had welcomed every new American into the Republican Volunteer Army. Who then lectured them during their training about scouting, reconnaissance, and the honest truth about how effective deceit is the most powerful weapon you can possess. Indeed, he was a pillar of theoretical wisdom who always wore his spectacles, making him look more academic than any of the teachers and students in the American Brigades, who made up no less than a third of their rosters. "Artillery support from behind us and central command informs me that our Russian friends are on the ready to help us from the air," he proclaimed from the highest platform possible in what had been, two weeks ago, a beautifully constructed

400-year-old stone villa. After delivering the rest of the speech, he moved on to where the horses had been gathered. He stroked the neck of the jet-black Andalusian Arab entrusted to Smith and his new girlfriend, Cervantes. "But these Comrades remain behind."

"Because?" demoted to infantryman Smith demanded to know.

"We have to cross the river first, and they can't swim or paddle boats as well as we can," Merriman related, instructing the lads behind him to distribute the remaining ammunition in the wagon to the platoon. "Which we will do successfully, gentleman." With that, Merriman put his hands behind his back and, with head held high, strolled to the next group of 'Lincolns.'

It was a convincing speech, which most of the platoon accepted as fact. And which the more analytical and brave thinkers in such pretended to accept as fact.

Such was observed from the top of the Republican side of the river by an observer with field glasses who could read lips. Cervantes could feel his or her presence, along with that of someone else who came up to him or her. "No, not spirits again, but intruders from our side of the veil, which is more dangerous," Carlos informed the terrified mare in Basque. "Just be sure that whatever happens, you, and your new jet-black Arabian friend, follow your own instincts and not the orders of any of us two-legged idiots and assholes."

With that, when the horse boys were not looking, Carlos leaned down and untied the hobbles binding her feet and that of the proud-cut gelding. He hoped they would have the sense, or luck, to run away from the lines so their bones could remain attached to their living heads instead of becoming meat for the vultures or stew for their starving owners, of which there was now no shortage, on the Republican and Nationalist side of the lines.

CHAPTER 10

The Republican charge up the hill on the other side of the river led by Merriman himself to liberate it from the Fascists was heroic, enthusiastic, and filmed by the best cinematographers Hollywood could provide. Being armed with righteousness, Determination, and being on the Right side of this War in which there really WAS a right and wrong side enabled the Lincoln Brigade to gain more ground than expected, even though the Republican artillery and Soviet air support promised to them had been absent. Indeed, the fully uniformed Nationalist battery that appeared deadly from the other side of the valley was, for the most part, silent, releasing scattered rounds at the advancing army that dwindled down into a spattering of missed shots that could be seen but barely heard. Small, then larger groups of low-ranking Nationalists retreated two 'trenches' back for every elevation in volume of the Internationale. The 'Come dressed as you are' Republican infantrymen sang as they advanced up the fortified mountain.   Republican pot shots mostly missed but sometimes did land into Fascist flesh.

"Maybe Franco's goons are considering asking their German and Italian advisors in the back lines for more money," John Smith said of the retreating Nationalist line. His aching forty-year-old feet and degenerating knees felt like they had been given a new lease on life mused to the two most trusted, hopefully, best known, men around him.

"Or listening to the words of the song," Vinny DeAngelo commented regarding the Internationale, an anthem that called for the end of slavery for those belonging to ALL classes, religions, colors, and nationalities. After singing the next stanza in Italian, he fired off five rounds. "One less 'master' left to oppress all of us," he smirked with delight as one of Franco's enlisted men fell to the ground, never to get up again. "Like shooting down wood ducks at Coney Island Amusement Park. Damn, am I good?"

"And could have done better if you got him in ONE shot or aimed at an officer," Tim Jackson interjected, noting the hard-on between Vinny's legs as the Wise Guy in training reloaded. "There's a shortage of ammunition down here and no shortage of Fascists up there."

"The Revolution doesn't pay us money; they can let us be compensated with a little fun, " Vincent replied as he prepared to take down another 'target' in the shooting gallery. "Besides, when we take that hill, we'll grab more ammo, some more food, some boots without holes in them, and a whole lot of souvenirs to take back home."

Smith worried about what Vincent meant by 'souvenirs.' He recalled stories about Mobsters in New York and soldiers in the Great War bringing home ears, eyes, scalps, and tongues of the slain, or still living, 'opponents.' But he was more worried about what Tim Jackson saw with worried eyes behind the field glasses.

"Order the men to attack faster," black 'private' Jackson 'advised' white 'Corporal' Smith, who, because of his age, use of academic speech, and the way he looked 'officerly' on a horse, was perceived of as a Lieutenant or Captain by five other platoons around him. "Attack faster; before the Fascists, we can't see now have time to set up machine gun nests or worse."

"More singing, and more firing, and more accurate firing!" Smith yelled out to the detachments to his right, left, and behind. "Now!" he yelled out in English and Spanish, feeling himself indeed to be a liberator worthy of sharing a steak dinner with his father in heaven or beans and rice with Carlos. That Basque commander was too far away on his right flank to give him approval of the order or an assessment of the mix of emotions behind it.

With that, Smith stood up and led three groups up the hill. Like confused mobs of travellers at train stations, following one passenger who seems to know what the right train track is, three more platoons followed as well. "Thinking and acting freely as 'one herd,'" Smith pondered, recalling the all too brief summers in his youth as a master cowboy herdsman. He was both liked and, in a strange way, respected by the cows, calves, and bulls under his stewardship.

Yes, belief in the right Cause was becoming a real victory! A God-given miracle in the service of humanity rather than the Pope, his Bishops, and Priests, along with their Capitalist Imperial secular moguls who believed that anyone who was rich and powerful was so because God ordained and blessed it. Those self-elevated mortals really did believe that the suffering of the working and peasant classes was something that was good for their souls and had to be amplified so they would get their reward in Heaven. As long as, of course, the Priests did not excommunicate them for being godless Communists or cheapskates who decided that their meager wages should go to feed their families rather than be donated to the Church.

Yes, the charge up the hill would, in a few magic moments, become a victory for Workers everywhere and the stop of Fascism here before it could spread everywhere else! Until…machine gun fire from hidden positions up the hill rained down from the Irish

Volunteers, the Portuguese regulars, Moroccan mercenaries, and Spanish Nationalists, who were well hidden from locations even Jackson couldn't identify. The attack sprayed deadly gunfire upon the Crusader Comrades, leaving a third of them dead and another third wounded.

Thankfully, most of the latter were able to crawl or be carried down to the river, then to the Republican 'trenches.' They were photographed there by freelance reports before being taken to the trucks and horse-drawn wagons to field hospitals elsewhere. In a battle that became…useless soon. Even for the Nationalist Fascists, who suffered just as many casualties and lost as many supplies as the Republicans did. And who, though still present in safe trenches, were able to secure land on both sides of the river, though in small patches which became…

"…..Strategically useless, for both sides, so I heard from one of the reporters who had informants on both sides of the river," one of the newest Republican mutineers protested to the three Comrade judges deciding his fate in the 'courtroom' set up in a cave converted into a courtroom. "You were sending us to our graves and not to glory! Aren't we free men fighting for freedom, choosing where and how we fight?"

"Yes, but," the head Spanish Republican judge replied through an interpreter. "But we have to punish you. For---"

----"Common sense, disloyalty or cowardice? Or not having enough stupidity to die for the Cause now instead of running away from a losing battle, so we can live to fight EFFECTIVELY another day!" replied Corporal, about to be demoted to the executed corpse, Smith, who had ordered a withdraw of the volunteers around him before still Colonel Merriman whistled a retreat for everyone. "We Americans are unilingual, ignorant about the world, and if left to our own devices, stupid, I know, but not expendable. Not this early in the War."

"But this is a War, and we have to punish you," the Judge shot back. "Just like George Washington shot deserters because he had to maintain loyalty and discipline."

"We all did what we could. Every member of the Lincoln Brigade."

"So why didn't you get shot? Like Comrade Merriman. Who got shot in the shoulder six times!" the judge pointed out.

"If not for me ordering and leading a retreat, he could have gotten shot in the head!" Smith shot back. "And the members of my platoon who got wounded, who I carried off No Man's land, would have wound up as breakfast for the rats, lunch for the vultures, or dinner for Fascists!"

"Yes, you were brave but insubordinate," the Head Judge said, after which he eyed over the now thirty mutineers, a quarter of which were guilty of not having an immune system that liberated them from the terror that had put them into catatonic shell shock. "We DO have to punish you, and the others here, for failure to do what the Republic and Revolution requires of all of us," he declared. He then turned to the other judges, both of which were larger in build but smaller in the muscles of assertiveness. "Right?" They nodded their heads, their eyes revealing that they were, or could have been, just as guilty of the offenses of being less than heroic legends as any of the accused.

"Therefore," the Head judge concluded, taking into his scarred three-fingered right hand a hammer, which he used as a gavel, preparing it to bang it on the empty ammunition box doubling as a desk. "This tribunal sentences you, Comrade Smith, and the others here to-----"

----"A chance to redeem themselves again," echoed through the cave from an intruder who seemed to appear from nowhere. "Do not judge, lest you be judged," Dimitri Pavlov declared in English, then Spanish as he stepped into the cave, proudly sticking out his medal-laden Soviet Army chest. "Comrade Jesus said that, and as we know, Jesus was a

Communist," he said to the interpreter in Spanish, which was then translated into English and French. Most of the prisoners had never seen combat before. Those who could still use their lips for talking instead of quivering translated Pavlov's declarations into languages their shell shocked countrymen could understand. "And Comrade Jesus said that we all sin, and all make mistakes and that we should support, understand and forgive the weaknesses in others, which are also in ourselves," Pavlov continued in a soft, passionate voice more in keeping with that of a compassionate psychiatrist than a highly decorated senior Soviet officer.

As for Smith, it was the first time that he heard a 'Godless Red' speak of the 'boss' of the Fascist-serving Clergy as 'Comrade Jesus'.

"Each gives according to their abilities and takes according to their needs. And since the Soviet Union is, besides Mexico, the only country that is GIVING instead of, like the French and Poles, SELLING you what you need," Pavlov continued, his hands behind his back in the manner of a serf-serving aristocrat who is sure of his position and purpose. He then turned to the Spanish judges. "We need and want you to release these Comrades without charges."

"And if they go to the enemy or run back home?" the Head Judge challenged.

Pavlov pulled in his lips, nodded his head, and then indulged himself in a chuckle of supreme confidence. "They won't do any of that," he asserted. "Will you, Comrades?" he requested of the mutineers.

A resounding 'no, Comrade, long live the Republic' came back from the first prisoner, a 22-year old olive skinned Mexican American with a more peach fuss than manly hair mustache sporting a wooded ring around his wedding finger, who pushed himself up upon his twisted left leg. The restraints of metal wire and ropes tied to his wrists were cut loose. He gave a 'comrade salute' to the Judge, who shot back a comrade salute and a stare that said 'Do this again, and it's the firing squad' in any language and was dismissed. Those who were not catatonic did the same, first individually, then in groups. As for those with shaking hands and eyes fixed in a blank stare, Smith turned to the Head judge. "Cowardice is a disease, not a crime," he said to the vengeance-seeking head Judge, as well as his two assistants, who feared for their lives if they offended Pavlov and his bosses.

"And you know a doctor who can treat this widespread malady, Comrade Smith?" Pavlov inquired of Smith in English.

"I think she can," the unarmed Smith replied, turning to the well-armed Soviet officer, facing him eye to eye. "She'll do her best anyway."

"Better than best," Smith heard from Tim Jackson as he appeared inside the cave, his teeth blasting into a blinding shade of white by the lantern illuminated by a wide smile. "Especially with the new commander of the Brigade, assigned by Merriman himself while he's recovering anyway. Comrade Hill!"

"A good man. A smart man," Pavlov noted. "And---"

"---A black one," Smith added.

"Who gave me Comrade Smith and a few of our Comrades? For a special assignment," Jackson informed the very Spanish White judge.

"And these Comrades are?" the judge shot back.

"In a hurry to get done what needs doin'," Tim Jackson added, taking it upon himself to untie the restraints on Smith. Who then raised his hand up in a fist, to the judge, then, after a tense delay, folded his elbow in the 'comrade salute' to him.

Reluctantly, the judge, then his two associates, returned the salute. With that, Pavlov bowed to the Revolutionary tribunal in the manner of a gentlemanly aristocrat from Pre-Revolutionary Russia, then left the cave. He was followed by Smith and Jackson, who escorted out the catatonic (and thankfully not shot) shell-shock victims. Their exploits in the war would remain nightmares in their heads rather than heroic tales told around the campfire at Scout Camp or fireplaces at universities designed to maintain the need for men to prove themselves in battle to become 'real men' at home.

CHAPTER 11

"Courage is being scared but somehow doing what you have to do, and when you DO do what you have to do, you will be the last one to smile with delight after it's done, if you smile at all," Sally recalled from her grandmother, a half Woods Cree and half Irish medicine woman who passed on her abilities as a healer, and her determination to help those in need before, and in preference to, those in want. As for healing those in need, there was no shortage of wounded in the church, which had been converted into a field hospital. Of course, that was after everything in it that was designed to glorify the Priests, the Pope, and (in that order) Jesus had been removed and converted to bandages, money to buy food for displaced civilians, and bullets for the wounded to use after they were deemed healthy enough to continue the fight. But there was one likeness of Jesus on the cross carved into the walls, which was not converted into firewood for sterilizing surgical instruments and fires to heat up rods to cauterize leaky blood vessels.

"So," Comrade Doctor Sally said as she wiped another thick layer of sweat-soaked blood from her forehead to the statue of the Savior on the cross, the most handsome likeness of him she had ever seen. This likeness of Jesus looked more like he was observing and assessing humanity rather than suffering for it. Taking a break from resuming a conversation with 'the Lord' she had called a halt to when she started to sprout breasts, she waved yet another three liters of wounded Comrades into the 'waiting room' of the overbooked operating room. "These men and women did their part to stop the evils of Fascism," she said to the 'J-man.' "Maybe you can have a talk with your Dad to help us out here? Or give Hitler, Mussolini, and Franco a brain, heart, and soul transplant? Or have them come down with the wounds, diseases and ailments that you seem to be 'testing' our Comrades with? Or turn the three Fascist machismo supermen into…" She found herself breaking into mad laughter while considering the next 'request.' "Yeah, turn the three Scrooges into…"

"…Nuns, who all get PMS at the same time, jealously fighting over who's going to get a 'special sacrament' from the village Priest," Captain Juan Fernandez suggested while passing by, yet again reading Doctor Sally's thoughts as well as offering her the possibility of expanding them. "A Fascist supported and funded Priest who…"

Sally yet again found refuge and a break from her masochistic brand of humanity, serving passion in her commander's tired yet still humor-embracing eyes. She felt that liberating infectious agent called comedy pushing up from her (despite the rumors) under-utilized female parts between her tired, shapely gams, lighting up every female and gender-neutral organ above it. The warmth of what some called love worked its way along with such into her stiff neck and slowly smiling lips.

"And once you docs turn the three Scrooges into Senioritas, we get us a priest who will make Sister Hitler cut off Sister Franco's 'Sieg Heiling' arm," an Irish Republican volunteer veterinarian-in-training who lost his right arm but not his life due to Sally's medical intervention bolted out with a smile as big as his homeland was green. "And give it to me so I can stick it up the ass and rip the guts out of Jimmy O'Donald and the rest of the Blue Shirts from Dublin who joined the Fascists," he pledged with an affirmative yet still painful rising of a fisted left forelimb.

"A priest who will chop the legs off the Fuhrer, Il Duce, and Generalissimo Franco, and make the one-legged trio fight for the honor of giving up the other one to the Temple of Apollo, the Alter of Odin or the chop suey pot at New Haven's Chinese Emporium," a new one and half legged Yale University football quarterback suggested. He had passed through the stages of shock, realization and anger, reaching 'action' somehow, no doubt envisioning how he would become an athlete with the muscle between the ears.

"Or a priest who convinces Hitler, Mussolini, and Franco to cut out one of their eyes and glue it to the back of their heads so they can see that most of their followers are really laughing at them. And have Jesse Owens running up behind them putting the final touches on am 'idiot and asshole of the year' Gold Medal on each of the 'fearless leaders' backs," a Baltimore-born and bred Negroid dock worker who was now a Negroid Comrade offered, as he adjusted the 'Pirate patch' over the hole which was occupied by a perfectly sound 20/20 eye three (unreported to the newspapers or history books) skirmishes ago.

All three heroes who were determined to go back to the battlefield looked at Sally, forcing smiles out of their lips begging her to laugh at their quips. She did her best to accommodate the men whose souls she connected to but whose names she didn't ask and couldn't remember anyway. She hoped that they would not see through her tired, bloodshot eyes into her burnt-out spirit and humor-starved soul. They would find out the secrets she was so good at hiding, so far anyway. Like that, every feature about her desirable to any red-blooded man's body seemed detestable to her on most days. And that though she was dedicated to saving lives here in Spain, rescuing people from death, or worse, it was just a job that fed her hungry soul with empty calories. And that she hated most of all receiving hugs of appreciation from any of her patients, especially the children. And that though the Harvard graduate received supplemental medical training from her backwoods Indian and industrial Irish grandparents in how to take a life in a street fight or international battlefield, she had never sent anyone to 'their just reward' herself.

Sally took in a deep breath of hot, humid air. Her nostrils detected rotting flesh, putrid blood, and booze from all over the world. Most of that firewater had been converted into both orally administered anesthesia for patients as well as antiseptic for surgical instruments. The distinct aroma of the international collection of alcoholic beverages reminded her of places she had been. And once loved relations who had surrendered their souls to 'Demon Rum,' who had themselves become demons. They were all memories of the past she would not go back to. They haunted her brain yet again. Until her shaking hand came in contact with something fresh, new, and, to the eyes, ears, and nose, beautiful.

"Lilacs, Comrade?" she recalled, eyeing Comrade Doctor Captain Fernandez approaching her as a Comrade beyond political affiliations. "My favorite flower, Juan," she continued with a smile from the heart that somehow penetrated into the brain. "And not just because it has healing properties for open wounds and can ease breathing in patients with anxiety, asthma, or allergy. But because…well…" The always somehow in-control superwoman looked at and into Fernandez's face, allowing herself to get lost in it. "How did you know they were my favorite flower?"

"I didn't, but he did," Juan replied, pointing to the shadow belonging to a man sporting a fringe buckskin coat, Mexican sombrero, and guitar cast upon the wall of the doorway to the church for the faithful now turned into a hospital that saved so many atheists and agnostics. He strummed a series of simple chords and harmonically dissonant bridge notes, which merged into a symphony of thirty different instruments in the ears within Sally's head, most particularly when she heard singing from the Spanish-speaking wounded from both sides of the Pond.

"And he is, Juan?" Sally inquired, recalling the men back home whose lives she had ruined or made more interesting, or both, in her 'experiments with blending in' to 'normal, pedestrian' peoples' realities. Perhaps it was one of her 'converts' to whom she delivered cures for dull-out disease that finally kicked in.

"He's a friend of the Revolution," Juan, as Comrade Fernandez, said. "Whose boss is a very rich and powerful friend of the Revolution who wants to--_"

"---See what we're doing here, in a Revolution and Army where, theoretically and ideally anyway, there are no bosses," she interjected, recalling that the poor, struggling country of Mexico had delivered more aid to the fight against Fascism here than any other 'civilized' country in Europe, or America. "What does this musical messenger's boss need? Besides further liberating his mind, of course."

"Someone to liberate his heart," Fernandez replied, after which he placed a card into Sally's hand from the gentleman caller emerging behind the solo musician. He first cast a shadow, showing himself to be clad in a non-musical trench coat, business suit, and fedora. The music from the Mexican Indian troubadour abruptly stopped, as did the symphony in Sally's head.

Sally looked at a note at the base of the Lilacs, daring not to show that she knew the dream patron's name. Her chest tightened with each syllable she read. Then she looked up at the gentleman's face as he slowly worked his way into the room, doing her best to hide her fear and disdain for him. "Comrade Doctor, we can be of great service to each other," the six-foot-tall businessman said with a courtly bow in a Tejano accent that was more Texan than Mexican to an ear familiar with life on either side of the Rio Grande. A Mexican trubador was behind him, strumming and singing Sally's favorite Sonoran love song.

Sally stared into his face with her trademark emotionless poker face. Her bottled-up anger, fear, and defiance increased with every movement of his increasingly upturned lips, which eventually fixed themselves into a smile.

"He looks familiar to you, Comrade Sally," the good, kind, and required-to-be effective Captain Doctor surmised, with mixed emotions.

"They all do, Doctor Juan," Sally finally whispered to him. "How did you find me here?" she thought of asking the city slicker ghost whose spit-shined shoes and suit had not a spot of dust on them but didn't. "I think he will find being here very uncomfortable, Comrade Captain," she said aloud to Fernandez. "The blood, the heat, the bombardments, the lice, the hunger, the diseases that spread around here---"

"---That he can provide medications to stop," Fernandez whispered back. He placed a list of items promised by the tall, handsome stranger into Sally's clenched fist. "With food, weapons, and everything else the Revolution needs," he continued. "And that these brave and hurting heroes and children need also," he whispered into her ear before she could come back with another one of her 'We have to keep the revolution pure, so it doesn't turn into another dictatorship' rants.

"All I ask is for a dance," the stranger bolted out with vulnerability in his voice and bravado in his eyes. "With the most beautiful lady in the room," he continued, his arms spread out like Santa on Christmas Eve. He motioned for his troubadour to begin strumming. Fernandez motioned for the 'patients' chorus' to sing along.

Every man and woman in the room motioned for the masochistic workaholic Doctor Sally (who could make everyone except herself else feel better, in big and small ways) to dance. Realizing that in a revolution based on democracy majority rules, particularly if it is a predominant majority, Sally accepted the dance with the 'stranger.'

"One dance, Jack," she whispered into his ear as he pulled her closer to her, showing off his skills as a dancer to Sally and the onlookers.

"Which ends when I say it ends, Mrs. Whittaker," Special FBI Agent Whittaker whispered back into Sally's ear in his natural North New Jersey accent. "And if you're wondering why you decided to marry me and stay with me, it's because you are a fugitive Communist masochist, and I am...well...a highly placed Capitalist sadist. Who you will work with and for, unless you want baby Ilene to, you know..."

"Yeah, I know," Sally replied, regarding the stepdaughter who she loved more than her father ever did, hiding her real emotions behind a smile so forced it was making her cheeks bleed.

CHAPTER 12

"The best indicator of how smart, effective, and intelligently compassionate a society is would be how it treats its prisoners," Captain Enrico Giamani thought to himself after being thrown back into the storage farm shack that had been converted into a prison cell for captured Italian soldiers. He wiped off the dust and hay from his Air Force uniform and shook the chains around his feet after having been interrogated by the Comrade Lieutenant Republican. "And what they serve us for dinner," the thirty-year-old aristocratic-born muscle-bound military protege said to a newly arrived fellow prisoner. Enrico's chained at the ankles but not between the ears. Army artillery officer cellmate was of equal rank and a bit lesser age, whose tattered blood-stained tunic seemed to be just as violated as his. His crotch lacked any urine stains, as did, of course, Giamani's.

Enrico sniffed the entrée left for him with his broken but still air-conducting nose. "Soup today, with some meat in it," he noted as he picked up a spoon with his aching black and blue hand, noting that the digits were still all there. "They said it was 'prime cuts' from the last Fascist military officer who refused to talk," he mused. "But it if was, I suppose it's alright since coward meat and heads are soft anyway. Not like mine, or...I hope yours," he said to his now and now only cellmate.

"But you must have told them something," Enrico's sole roommate noted, inviting him to sit down next to him on the hay bail, his chains digging into his ankles.

"Yes, I did," Enrico related with downturned eyes. He tasted the stew, slurping it into the recesses of his uninjured left lip. "I did tell them that I would consider the idea of joining them," he said after tasting the meat and still green vegetables, pushing it through his throat with more ease than his previous meals at the 'grey bar hotel.' "If I could get a kiss from Comrade Stalin, with HIM wearing the dress," he mused. "After I get to shave off his mustache and cut off his balls, if he has any."

"Which bought you another punch in the jaw," Enrico's fellow Blackshirt added. "And that got me this." He rolled up his sleeve, showing with pride a deep slash in his right upper arm that seemed partially healed, with two matching recently obtained scars below the rib cage.

"Nasty," the hard-bitten pilot, whose tolerance for pain was as high as the altitudes he flew at, winced. "Those papercuts and bruises look painful."

"We were both trained by El Duce to endure a lot more in the service of fighting the godless Communists in the Cause of Law and Order," the artillery officer said, extending his right hand, which contained bandages on what was no doubt a missing fourth and fifth digit to Enrico, slipping into a Southern Italian accent. "I'm Josepi Baldino…and you are…"

"Enrico…Giamani," the Palermo-born pilot said with his extended still finger bearing right hand to his fellow person and patriate, with more admiration for an artillery officer he never had extended or felt. "And what brought you here?"

"Unexpected firepower from Russian airplanes, and a barrage of crazy Republicans on foot, Giamani," Josepi replied. "And you?"

"I swooped down too low while doing a reconnaissance run. I was shot down, so they claimed, by two teenaged kids with rifles, Josepi" Enrico related. "Maybe I should have been smarter than braver."

"Which serves us well here, Giamani," Josepi said, pointing through the barred window to the recently re-captured 400-year-old villa now occupied by Republicans who had no appreciation for the artwork inside and less for the Deity who those frescos and paintings glorified. "It's a golden opportunity to give them false information," Josepi suggested. "Which, of course, we have to hold back until they think they've broken us. We tell those overly armed, under-aged Commie brats and deluded idiots fairy tales they want to hear, which backfire on them. Like that, we are stuck with no ammunition forty miles to the North with only 200 starving conscripts."

"When you have 2,000 well-armed trained soldiers who will massacre them when those cowards try to take the town, thinking it's easy pickings," Giamani added with a confident smirk. "Which I did also in there, according to our training," he continued. "I told them that we're planning a major assault from the East no earlier than three days from now."

"When you're about to attack from the West in two days, Enrico?" Josepi appended.

"With crack, well-armed troops, including Moroccan mercenaries, in less than 24 hours, at night," Giamani added, after which he took another bite of the stew. "Who will be singing the Internationale on their trek through the woods? Sung also by chained Republican prisoners who will be our body shields. And if those prisoners decide to try to run away or give us away, we kill their wives, children, or, even more frightening to them, 'Comrade' mistresses."

"Good plan, Enrico," Josepi nodded, after which he limped up from the 'dining room table,' clanking the chains restraining his feet. He treated himself to a glance of three truckloads of more Republicans coming into the camp, singing songs of victory in languages Enrico did not understand nor wanted to. "We should be liberated from these hobbles soon then."

"And the stupidity of that cowardly and stupid Basque Lieutenant commander, who thinks he is a master interrogator, Josepi," Giamani mused. "And I'll personally fly you back to Rome, or Berlin to see that you get the medal you deserved for having balls and brains."

"Yes, Enrico," Josepi replied, turning back to his roommate. "But in the meantime..." he retrieved a bottle of vino from a loose board on the floor of the shack. "I wish it were the blood from those Communists demons, but it will get us through the night. And their victory infernal singing!" Josepi poured the elixir into two metal cups, offering one to his guest. "To...victory in battle, Enrico."

"And the song, Josepi!" Giamani said as he lifted up the glass to his mildly parched and, to be truthful, only mildly bloody lips.

It was the best wine Giamani had tasted in Spain since he left his native Sicily. And in the best of company. He heard his host sing 'Facetta Nera,' the 1935 tune about liberating Ethiopian women by giving them a new Italian king, with an accent that sounded a bit different than expected. But then again, with wine, any strange accent becomes familiar and native to the listener. The duo sang out in harmony the tune which cajoled then inspired so many adventures and girl-seeking boys to become accomplished men in the service of the new Italian Empire that would last longer than Rome's did, and with less trouble from upstart inferior races and freedom fighters.

By the fifth chorus, Enrico closed his eyes and fainted into a blissful sleep, falling onto the lap of his drinking and operatic companion. The door was suddenly opened up from the outside. A bright light shone into Josepi's face. He addressed the silhouette of a tall man who stood at the doorway.

"So, 'Josepi,' what did you get from 'Enrico'?" now Lieutenant Carlos Garcia inquired of Vinny DeAngelo, looking at the passed-out corpse of the toughest, most intelligent, and manipulative young officer in the Italian Armed forces.

"A lot more than you fucking did," Vinny replied, pushing the happy and dumb clam drunken Fiat pilot off of his lap, then spitting into his arrogant Fascist face. "It's easier to trick your enemy into telling you the truth than torturing them into telling you a lie. And like my old man says, keep yer friends close, your enemies closer. And…." His next thoughts were held hostage in his throat by the pain in his arm and chest.

"No matter how much it hurts, don't let anyone hear you say…OUCHH!" he grunted.

"But remember," Carlos said. "That those wounds on your hand you got fighting for the Right side at Jamara are medals of honor that no one can take away from you."

"Yeah," Vinny grunted, lifting up his right hand and giving the third-digit salute to Giamani. "I can still give you this!" he yelled out regarding one of the only three digits left on that hand. "And now that you're fucking usefulness to us is done with this!" he continued, pulling a revolver out of Carlos' holster. "And this!" Vinny yelled out, pointing the barrel into the ace pilot's mouth. "And with the fingers I still have, I can give you this!"

Before Carlos could stop him, Vinny clicked the trigger, developing a hard-on with each progressive uplifting of the edges of his outer lips. Nothing came out from the first chamber or any of the other five. Pushing Carlos aside and then into a painful thump on the wall, Vinny grabbed hold of the Basque's knife and proceeded to stab Giamani in the chest multiple times, awakening him from his blissful slumber and then sending him into a sleep he would never wake up from while muttering curses in Italian that Carlos didn't know, or want to know. The Italian-born New Yorker class clown who was the best morale officer in the Lincoln Brigade, or perhaps any other Brigade, had lost the ability to make hurting civilians and fellow comrades. Laugh, sing, or even smile.

Carlos somehow restrained his own urge to deliver corporal payback to Vinny or to say, 'fuck, this really does hurt' regarding his own battle wounds and now aching back. He retreated into his head again. Was the 'wet-behind-the-smart-assed-ears' 19-year-old becoming this strange kind of man because of being shot, shooting others, or seeing what war was doing to others, most particularly the kids whose childhood was taken away by the War, never to be returned? Still, Vinny was a unique tool for the Cause. What kind of tool? That was another matter entirely, as unpredictable to the usually accurately calculating Basque Lieutenant in the Spanish Republican Liberation Army as the roll of the dice at the crap table. Or determining the odds of who gets hit by cannon fire or bullets in any cavalry charge, no matter what horse you are riding. But he did know all too well that the easiest target to hit and kill is anyone who is retreating.

CHAPTER 13

The orders entrusted to a recently clean-shaven 'Sister' Carlos were simple. "Take three small locked chests from Sally's mostly American hospital near Segovia with white-whiskered 'Father' Vincent riding shotgun. Proceed by horseback alongside, but never on the roads en route, with branches on the tails of the firm footed by aging nags behind you. Deliver the chests to a boat landing 10 miles west of Gijon and pick up five large boxes to be driven by horse-drawn carts on the same route. Do not stop for anything or anyone, and complete the delivery with haste. If stopped or captured, blow up the chest boxes, then yourselves. Spare the horses if you can. And above all, do not open the chests or the boxes." They were simple orders from the High Command. But there were some things that High Command didn't anticipate for the hand-picked men to get through Fascist-held territory unnoticed.

"Hey! You said these horses were fucking bomb-proof!" Vincent said as the lead steed pulled his head up unexpectedly, heading for a run away from a fire that suddenly burst up from behind a thicket of trees in the distance. "And that you knew how to handle anything on four hoofs better than anything on two legs!" he yelled out as the reins nearly slipped out of Carlos' hands.

"Stop!" Carlos assertively requested in five European tongues, as neither he nor Vincent knew the national origin of the stray horses. But the runaway team headed down a wide mountain road fraught with more bumps, recently dug fox holes, and bits of metal that were probably land mines.

"They gotta stop! Make them fucking stop!" Vincent yelled out to Carlos. He held on to the cross around his neck while the wind blew open his unbuttoned Cossack, creating a flapping that made the horses even more terrified. "Make them fucking stop!" he blasted up to the sky.

"Stop making them go faster first," Carlos grunted through the side of his mouth, pulling off Vincent's Cossack and throwing it into the wind, a Republican Army uniform underneath it. Worn so that, if captured, he would be sent to a prison camp or perhaps back home to 'neutral' America rather than be shot as a spy.

With his soothing Basque singing voice, Carlos sang a lullaby intended to calm down Vincent as much as the horses. It prevented a runaway into a narrower portion of the secluded meadow leading to a steep drop off which had not been there on the way back to yet another headquarters which they called 'home'. The horses were still at full gallop, but at least they were on flat ground now. Up ahead was a hill, which de-escalated the gallop to a sort of controlled lope, then a brisk trot. 'Sister Carlos' turned to a terrified and explative-blasting Father Vincent. "That Spirit you call God, who maybe you just started talking to now, made that hill so horses could slow down," Carlos said. "But---". The fastener on his Nun's habit loosened, causing it to slap against his stubbled face, blinding him and putting the horses into a swift gallop once more.

Vincent grabbed hold of the reins with his fully fingered hands. Then, with the other one, he pulled on 'Sister Carlos' habit, ripping it off the Basque, then letting the wind take it. With brains in his hands he never knew he had, the Brooklyn-raised street kid whose only experience with horses had been betting on who was the fastest at Bellmont Park somehow got the steeds to halt just before they reached the summit of the hill in a thicket of bushes. He breathed a sigh of relief, and self observed himself doing the sign of the cross. "Thank you!" he muttered.

"For our help, not 'the Good Lord's,'" Vincent heard in a high-pitched voice from a rider in a uniform he didn't recognize, with an even crown of cropped hair and some bruises on the scalp. "And what were you doing in 'these,'" the heavily armed rider continued. Another recently shorn soldier in a similar but not identical uniform appeared behind the wagon, shaking 'Father Vincent's' Cossack with one hand and Sister Carlos' habit with the other. A third rider emerged, aiming the business end of a Tommy gun at Vincent and his companion. "You came 'back home' in the service of the Lord?"

"We're here in the service of humanity," Carlos interjected, pointing to his Republican uniform, then Vincent's before the Brooklynite mobster in training could utter a creative lie that probably would not be appropriate. "And what brings you Comrades here?" Carlos inquired of the three heavily armed riders.

"Revenge for this," the head rider, who upon closer examination was a young woman, said, pointing to her shaved head. "And worse things the Fascists did to my sisters, mother, daughter. And now my fellow Anarchists' husbands and brothers."

"We've taken back the town," the second rider, a shorn shield maiden with an even more feminine face, informed Carlos.

"And invite you both to a bonfire," the third rider' smiled. With the utmost delight, she pointed her angry fingers towards the town, where the tallest building was ablaze. She led Vincent and Carlos in for a closer look. A large metal cross held itself firm somehow above the flames. The church's bell fell to the ground, disappearing in a cloud of black smoke. Screams begging for mercy could be heard from clergy of both genders as they were thrown against a wall by a mob that had cornered, beaten, and scalped other Priests and Nuns to equal extents. After a resounding chorus of 'tres, duo, uno' from the glee-infected mob, another round of gunshots could be heard behind the smoke, sending the clergymen and women on to the afterlife to join the other corpses clad in Holy Robes and Nationalist Military uniforms. In front of the bonfire being fueled by another round of wooden icons were 200-year-old paintings, holy robes, Bibles, and prayer benches, as well as several not-yet-dead corpses. Gold and silver icons were thrown into another pile for collection by the 'officer' Anarchists, who distributed some to the poor, some into trucks for evacuation, and some for themselves. As the 'band played on'.

"They burned Pagan earth healers as witches. Now it's their turn to face the fires of hell," the head Anarchist rider proclaimed. "As a Basque, you should appreciate that," she directed to Carlos.

"We converted the Fascist-run Churches into hospitals," Carlos shot back, holding back his anger, directing it through as much applied reason as he could muster in the middle of the chaos. "And we, by law, disallowed the priests and nuns to be teachers in any school. We did it by democratic law!"

"Which was not effective enough to stop them!" the militant head rider reminded the Basque 'wannabe pacifist.' "You are in Anarchist country now, Comrade. And..isn't it true that a thousand churches and clergy are not worth one Republican life?"

"To some of us, yes," Carlos related and confessed.

"Including me," Vincent asserted. He held back the details of his history with the 'good fathers' and 'blessed Mother Superiors' back home in the high schools that were well funded to teach their delinquent students 'good manners and better morals.' "After they did to me…and my brother what…"

"---Deserves jail time, not castration or hanging," Carlos interjected.

"What's in those boxes?" the head rider inquired of the locked crates.

"Some shit we're are supposed to deliver to People's Revolution Headquarters, which, on last account, is still outside of Segovia," Vincent replied, in his best Spanish, of course not being 'faggy' enough to say such with a lisp.

"Which is here now," the head Anarchist in the Woman's Liberation brigade barked out, after which she shot open the locks on the 'not to be opened' crates. A single note lay upon dust-covered rifles, modern weapons that bore Russian writing. "' To be handled only by the most dedicated enemies of Fascism,'" she read. "Which is now us," she asserted, reaching for the largest and most insensitively technical of the submachine guns.

"No!" Carlos barked out, knocking the woman on her ass, then noting with his nose the odor of the white powder on her hands. She began to cough. Blood poured out of her mouth. Her breaths got shorter and more desperate. "That powder is toxic!" he warned them regarding that latter most unexpected finding. "And as for the inscription on these weapons," he continued, gazing at the inscriptions, sensing something even more unexpected and sinister. "Russian letters that are backward."

Vincent put on a pair of gloves and examined one of the rifles. "And rifles that fire backward with more bang than forwards," he noted. He demonstrated the point by putting a round of bullets into one of the heavier machine guns, aiming the barrel at a tree, and firing it, keeping both ends of the weapon two feet to his left. A trajectory of shrapnel reduced a tree trunk behind him to bits of bark. "An old trick the shithead cowboys did when they sold guns to the Injuns," he said to Carlos, who translated such to the Spanish ladies in arms.

"And what about her?" rider two asked of head rider, the skin around her mouth and nose white coated with the toxic powder, those orifices spewing out blood. Anarchist three dismounted and desperately rushed to her leader's aid.

Carlos lifted the head anarchist into the wagon while she begged the God she claimed didn't exist for help. "Maybe my Earth Healer can help her," Carlos said to her two compadres. "No doctor anywhere else can if this power is what I think it is. What's her name?"

"Maria," the second rider replied, having finally gotten her chance to be promoted to platoon commander in the last way she ever wanted to be.

"And her fellow Anarchist Comrade?" Carlos inquired of rider 3, whose concern for the intoxicated leader was far more intimate and special than that of being a fellow soldier in any Cause.

"Teresa," came from the quivering lips of the new "Sargent" of the Anarchist detachment, with a tear from her eye. "Who---" she continued, unable but wanting to talk about the depth of her relationship with Maria.

"---We will take care fucking good care of as well and use in Common Cause," Vincent interjected, Carlos translating.

The second rider did not prefer to give her name. Instead, she retrieved Maria's rifle and then mounted her horse. "Go with God," she said in Spanish. "Who is with us atheists, not the good Catholics or the communion-taking Fascists!" she proclaimed, after which she rode into the liberated town. Leaving Vincent and Carlos concerned not only about the fate of Maria but also the reason why they were sent on a secret mission to retrieve boxes of toxins and weapons intended to kill Republicans rather than Fascists.

CHAPTER 14

"So, we give you a chest full of money, and you come back with…this?" now (due to two of his superiors' deaths), Colonel Comrade Doctor Fernandez slurred to Vincent and Carlos after opening up the wagon upon their return to the seminary which had been converted to the Northwest sector communication center. And, in the hopes that it would prevent bombings from above, a Red Cross referral hospital. "An anarchist with, so I heard, the unauthorized blood of Nuns and Priests on her hands," Carlos related regarding the patient in his wagon.

"An anarchist who is in need of special attention, who killed more Fascist soldiers yesterday than you did all week, named Maria," Theresa blasted back at Fernandez regarding her fellow liberator. Maria's only reason for still being able to pass air from her bloody mouth to her raspy lungs was the fact that she had caressed and sung to her for the last 20 bumpy, rocky, and wet miles by Theresa. With a crowbar, Theresa would have preferred to use ram the regular Republican Army commander's ass, and she opened the false bottom on Carlos' cart. "Whose medical bills will be paid for with these!" she blasted into the oculars below his rolling eyebrows, treating him to a view. "The latest in weapons from the Italian, German, and Irish Republican Army, which we Anarchists captured!"

Vincent filled Fernandez in on the official names and year of production of the armaments. Then, the nicknames their former users had given to the weapons that Teresa and Maria had taken from the Nationalists under, officially anyway, Republican Spanish command. Such Fascist technical terminology included Comrade Castrators, Socialist Slashers, and Communist Cancer Extractor. "We got twenty of them while passing through two villages the Anarchists liberated, along with fresh horses stolen back from Franco's goons," Vinny continued.

"And the ninety Russian, French, and Mexican guns you were supposed to pick up?" Fernandez pressed.

"Most of them we left behind in enemy territory," Carlos replied regarding the weapons and 'medicated' hand powder sent by smugglers who had run the blockade to help the revolution. Smugglers who were working for the other side. The enraged and insulted Basque threw his former friend, and now boss, one of the booby-trapped weapons picked up at the beachhead. "So they could shoot themselves instead of us." He demonstrated how they were designed to spray shrapnel into the face, eyes, and neck of the shooter.

"With toxic gunpowder, they could use to keep their balls dry if they didn't blow their heads open," Vincent added, handing the impressed but ungrateful Spanish Colonel a bag of collected powder. "If too much of it gets on your hands, you lose fingers," he related, lifting up Maria's shooting arm bearing only two functional digits. "If too much of it gets into your lungs…" he continued, pointing at Maria.

Carlos related the Spanish name of the toxic component of the 'hand powder' to Fernandez.

"Which none of my family in New York or Sicily used on any of our competition if they took territory that wasn't fucking theirs. Or even any fucking low life who ratted us out, so I heard anyway," Vinny replied as he pulled off a Nun's habit, which he, so he claimed, kept on his head to keep the Nationalist troops from identifying him while taking short cuts through their territory. And to shelter himself from the hot sun and cold rain. He sniffed the air in the camp, and It oozed off freshly cooked stew rather than putrid infected blood. "And speaking of rats," Vincent said. "Someone paid something big for room service. Maybe someone who---"

"---So where is Doctor Comrade Sally, Comrade Carlos!?" Theresa demanded to know before any fingers, be they intact or falling off a hand, could be pointed at anyone. "You said, and promised, that she could save my… friend!" She made her determination clear on the matter by pulling out a revolver from her non-caressing, aiming it at Carlos, Vincent, and the Republican Commander of matters medical and, without his consent, military. "Tell me where the miracle witch is, or I'll---"

"---Do something that no one can fix," Sally said as she appeared behind Teresa in a more blood-stained than the clean white surgical gown, accessorized by bloodshot eyes that had not seen nightmares or dreams for two days. She took a whiff of the toxin, then the patient. "We'll start with this," she said, retrieving a spray bottle from the oversized handbag slopped on her shoulder. After three sprays into Maria's through and a quick, somehow remorseful prayer in a language neither Vincent nor Carlos recognised, Maria's agonizing death rattle gave way to breathe that easily passed from her chest to her mouth, putting a smile on the latter.

"An offering to Spirit big S, and as for the subtext of it, being Catholic makes you apologize for rain. And being Pagan makes you apologetic for not being Catholic enough," Sally provided by way of a multifactorial explanation. "But, as for now, as always," she said as she helped Teresa bring Maria into the chapel where people had prayed for good health into a hospital where they actually DID get such. "Heaven watches, earthworks."

"That means in English---" Carlos slurred from the side of his mouth to Vincent.

"---God helps those who fucking help themselves," the Italian American Wiseguy who was becoming wiser than he bargained for retorted. "And when the angels are still on a lunch break."

"We hire demons?" Carlos inquired, searching for which moral compass was guiding Vincent's too-well-trained-for-his-own good mind-soul.

"Outlaws," Vincent blasted back. "Who doesn't trust anyone."

"Except each other," Vincent heard from behind him. "Comrade," Smith continued, patting him on the back.

"And the press, from the wrong newspapers," Comrade now Lieutenant Tim Jackson added.

"And who is going to get help from the right ones," emerged from a face and voice that seemed familiar to Vincent.

"Hey…you're…eh…" Vincent asked of the American whose non-odorous body aroma, trimmed mustache, intact non-military clothing, and non-emaciated belly revealed him to be in a position of political power here. Or maybe he was someone who had just come off the boat in Beiritz. "I know you from somewhere. You…"

"---Wrote that 'heroism, bravery, and smarts are something that overtakes you, when you least expect, or want it to,'" he offered as he strolled up to Vincent. He retrieved a flask from his black leather coat. "Something that happened to me in the First World War, and you already proved in this second one," he said as he offered Vincent a swig from it, along with his business card. He motioned for an attractive, small-framed woman with a big, ugly camera to approach a car that had its fair share of bullet holes in it. "Can my photographer take a picture of me and your Comrades?"

Vincent was still in the dark as to who this journalist was now working for the New York newspaper, which, relative to the other rags back home, printed more truth than bullshit. But Tim Jackson, John Smith, and Carlos rushed in front of the camera after seeing who it was. "And Sally!" the famous writer whose words Vincent recognized yelled out towards the hospital. "Whose picture---"

"---You got already, back in France when we got off the boat, and at the peer in New York?" she assertively inquired out, with anger, desperation, and…shame. The latter emotion is something that surprised Vincent.

"And won't get again until SHE is ready," came from…yes, Maria in a clear, distinct voice between coughs.

"OK then," the reporter who Vincent now recognized as one of the top novelists in America. Whose books he sort of read when he was in the clink. And who would maybe find his way into another one of his books? Hopefully not as a hero who was fond of cross-dressing as he was dedicated to doing the right thing.

Vincent distanced himself from the nun's outfit he had worn as 'camouflage and the female gestures he had adopted to make such convincing on his last Mission. He smiled for the camera, the lady photographer, and the folks back home. As did his Commie black, rebel Basque and WASP Iowan compadres. He indulged himself with another issue as he heard music emerge from the mess hall. Who would get the first dips on the booze in his flask, and who would get the first dance with the photographer lady?

CHAPTER 15

The three-month tour of duty, honor, and redemption anticipated by most of the Lincoln Brigade went into the fifth month, as measured by long stretches of boredom punctuated by brief periods of terror. For the younger idealistic American Crusaders in the fight against Fascism, much of it was a cultural adventure. This was particularly true with Spanish women who had lost their husbands who had loved them and the widows' fathers who protected them from men who loved them in the wrong way. For thinking idealists who had the luxury or curse of having survived past thirty, such as John Smith, it was about his ever-changing relationship with his shifting political belief systems and, of course, God. That Deity's presence seemed to be erratic at best with regard to showering down from His place in the sky, workable weather, and luck on the battlefield. It was also true for seasoned black veterans of the Great War of 1917-8, such as Tim Jackson, who completely forgot what skin tone they had inherited in an environment where all men and women shed the same color of blood. In this war against Fascism, each day had become a soul-numbing 'just another day at the office,' where, of course, every day involved the disappearance of some of his co-workers at such.

From his vantage point on top of a hill overlooking the valley where a new offensive was due 'any time now,' Jackson glanced at a convoy of trucks pulling in. "I hope the hell these trucks have more assets than liabilities in them, people and weapons wise, John," 'Comrade Tim' (as the Captain preferred and insisted on being called) asked his WASP compadre while he did last-minute repairs on the latest machine gun sent by 'Santa Stalin' nestled amidst whatever brush hadn't been blown up. "But these new men look healthy anyway."

"The women, too," John added, pointing Tim's attention to aired trucks in another portion of the convoy. "Who, by the way, they're carrying themselves, and their grandfather's vintage rifles and grandmother's kitchen knives, look like they are here to fight Fascists rather than entertain the men or nurse the wounded. And…most of them still have their long hair, which…hmmm…" He placed field glasses in front of his bloodshot eyes. He smiled with the kind of delight that almost matched those occasions when the shower truck came by to spray off the layers of lice and dirt from his aging-faster-than-he-anticipated body, providing a fresh set of clothes and a hot meal afterward. "One of them in particular who is very much a woman, speaking French," John went on. "A real…hmm…No, THE mademoiselle from Armateers. Like my father…hmmm…maybe met before he…"

"He gave his life for a noble Cause?" Tim offered with an assuring bearlike hand on the WASP shaking, small and thankfully not yet shot into piece shoulder. "Like you giving a PORTION of your life to THIS Cause," he continued, feeling then seeing John slip into guilt again. Tim held back, of course, the truth that the millions who died in the Trenches did so in the service of Capitalists on both sides of the War who got fat, rich, and very comfortable during that 'War to End All Wars.' "Yes, this war we're in now is as noble as wars come and is completely necessary. One that we fight for---"

"---The women back home?" John interjected, his attention held hostage by the French bombshell with the long braid of flaming red hair who was as beautiful as, according to the collection of medals over her left breast, brave. His daytime dream was quickly ended by recalling the woman he had left back home. "In my case, a sheltered, empty-souled, superficial wife," he said regarding the dream babe he should have left at the alter instead of taking a sabbatical from his marital duties after having three children with her. "Who…maybe I don't want to go back to. Who I thought, when we married, was someone else….Who…"

"You thought it was her?" Tim offered, referring to the French beauty in his sights, taking the field glasses away from John. "Who you can't have."

"Why!" John protested.

"Because she was mine," Tim asserted. A smile came to his tired and, all things considered, still not disfigured face. The business end of his spyglass somehow the face then blue eyes of the forty-years-young ageless beauty. The only evidence of her advancing years were crow's feet around her eyes. But they made her seem even more beautiful than her wrinkled female comrades on the inside and the outside. "Yeah. She was mine a long time ago and…"

"Can it be again?" John inquired.

Tim felt the WASP midwesterner seeing and evaluating but not judging his past history with her.

"Jenell!" Tim shouted out, standing up on his blister-covered feet. Every element of tension in his chest converted into thunderbolts of joy that flashed into his fingers, legs, and spine.

"Tim!" Jenell shouted back, after which she ran up the hill. She spoke to Tim in French to her old flame. But when Tim looked away to revisit memories behind his ocular portions, she unexpectedly started an even deeper non-verbal conversation with John with her eyes…

CHAPTER 16

After becoming a military doctor who saved lives as well as a soldier who took them, Comrade Doctor Juan Fernandez knew all too well that when flesh has a battle with metal, metal always wins. And when wood meets metal, the breakdown of the former is all the more intense and rapid, particularly in the hands of a chopper who has an axe to grind. He knew better than to ask Sally why, during a cool month when no bombs could be heard, and the only patients coming into the hospital were those with mild cases of venereal disease or wounds obtained in bar fights, she busied herself with the most exhausting work available. It pained Fernandez in ways he had never experienced to see her sweating bullets while converting logs into burnable firewood with more intensity than Beethoven probably had when banging on the piano to pound out a tender sonata and hear SOME of the notes with his failing ears.

Sally was more than entitled to have a well-deserved and High Command-ordered fortnight of rest and recreation. Gentle walks by the now NON-bloodstained river with him. Or time to write fantasy-infused poetry and prose, which made any reader think, feel, and laugh. But as Juan Fernandez was told by the Spirit Messenger in his dreams, 'intensity was Sally's life, and it would kill her.' "Gotta die of something," he told himself as he watched her putting ten men and twenty women's strength into chopping the fallen trees into burning logs and kindling, tossing them into a stockpile higher than any hill within 2 miles. "And I suppose that if you intensely try to solve problem A, the solution for problem B will materialize," he recalled from his own experimentations with masochistic workaholism.

Juan thought of reminding Sally that the more splinters that found their way into her fingers and vibrations of the axe that would make her tendons scream with irreparable inflammation, the less effectively she would be able to use them for fast, effective surgery when the War came back around to this, for this precious God-given time, peaceful valley. And that her skills as a translator of books and player of music on the piano were far more needed than a mountain of firewood and kindling that would not be needed until summer gave way to winter again. But Juan had to say something to the formerly charismatic genius who was not only a credit to her gender but the human race in general.

"You look thirsty," he said, offering her a canteen of fresh, cool water.

"I am thirsty," her reply, averting his eyes. She focused on a demon inside the next proudly solid log, which was about to surrender to the destructive energy in her hand. With one large swing, the chunk of a fallen tree that Mother Nature had formed into something far more artistic than any carved statue was broken into slivers in a thunderous roar, which was only matched by Sally's ear braking growl of conquest.

Both startled a ten-year-old recently orphaned girl from Catalina who had, less than a week ago, found a new purpose and a reason to smile by assisting Sally in the OR, aspiring to be 'just as artistic and scientific' as she was. "What's wrong, Doctor Maestro Sally?" Helena asked from a safe distance. "You want me to help?"

"No! Not from a child your age with your...." Sally slurred out of the side of her mouth with whatever humanity she had left as she continued to demolish a very appropriately sized piece of log into more useless kindling.

"With my what?" Helena asked, begging for an honest answer.

"Just go away! The last thing I need is another child who..." Sally replied, hiding her face and real agenda for doing anything from both Juan and Helena.

"She's just having a rough time on that time of the month that you will have to experience in a few years," Juan said as he knelt down to wipe the tears streaming down from Helena's sorrowful eyes before the face under them could turn beet red with unstoppable anger. He looked behind him to Sally, prepared to get an angry retort regarding PMS, which would be directed at him rather than Helena, the wood, or anyone else who offered a kind hand to her. "Yeah, that time of the month," he continued, bracing his ears for a scream that would have behind it the real answer as to why, ever since the American Philanthropist had come into Camp and country, she was...' different.' Since that fateful visit from the 'American Cavalry', Sally never really looked into anyone's eyes, especially the person who she saw whenever she bypassed a mirror.

Sally held the axe in her hand, looking at the next piece of wood to chop up with a serene and remorseful apology. "That time of month lasts 30 days now," Sally informed Helena in perfectly accented Spanish. "So leave me the fuck alone and stop trying to cure me of whatever disease you think I have. And stop trying to make me care for or value anyone else," she went on to Juan in Russian, disguising the subtext with a mild, pleasant demeanor.

Juan turned to Helena, prepared to translate into Spanish a message and comment about life that was kinder than Sally's 'discourse' and the meaning behind it. But before he could open his mouth to provide an already over-traumatized Helena with something that would heal her wounds and lead her to not only survival but good, enjoyed health of the body, mind, and spirit, the little wonder-seeking girl instantly grew up, aging 10 years in as many seconds. She was transformed into a bitter, cynical 'I go through life because I have to, not because I want to' woman. "Papa was Russian," she said to Juan in her father's native tongue. "And my mother told me that only a fool expects love from someone who doesn't love you. Smart people do unto others before they get done unto." With that, she stormed away, a frown of resignation on the face Doctor Sally had repaired medically, which was now as sorrowful as it was biologically beautiful.

Juan tortured himself with alternating long stares at Helena and Sally. A thought came to his aching and nearly sun-stroked head. At the core of Sally's anger, guilt and masochism was one element. Prior to this awakening that happens to all people in War, Helena had been…a child just like Sally must have been at one time, perhaps. Or perhaps not.

CHAPTER 17

"So, Comrade Carlos, tell me again why we were assigned to work together?" Vinny DeAngelo asked as he felt yet even more aching ass hit the saddle harder with each bumpy stride through the woods.

"You and that horse, or you and me?" Basque Captain Carlos proposed from the back of a bay Polish Arab mare who had miraculously survived having three previous riders being shot dead off of her. All three riders had been from different sides of the War, the Nationalists, the Republicans, and the 'leave me the fuck alone' third portion of the Spanish population. "We're here because of Orders, from the top again from—"

"—Comrade Colonel Tom Hill? The Black commander of the Lincoln Brigade who has it in for white WAPs?" Vinny barked back.

"Higher," Carlos answered.

"Comrade General Luis Serrano, the Spanish General of the Republicans?" Vinny slurred out between grunts of pain in his ass, preferring the pain of foot blisters and inflamed ankle tendons the Infantry was privileged to enjoy.

"Higher," the Basque philosopher-soldier replied. "President Doctor Professor Juan Negrin."

"The civilian Comrade president?" Vinny barked back. "Who pins these medals on my chest and rewards me with more 'on a need to know basis' explanations for the next job I'm 'uniquely qualified' to do, instead of giving me two fucking weeks off so I can steal a goddamn boat, find out what Italian 'education camps' my uncles and real Godfather are in so I can finally fucking—"

"—Educate the fucking guards with the business end of a fucking bayonet?" Carlos blasted out so loud that he scared both horses. "Then single-handedly, you let every member of 'the family' out of their fucking cells and sneak them out of the camps so they can plan and execute a fucking contract on Mussolini? Kill that motherfucking law and order asshole who made the fucking trains run on time? And if we fucking pay them enough, hire police hitmen to off a Franco and Hitler?"

Holding onto the reins of his spooked horse for dear life, Vinny felt his jaw drop, unable to reply to Carlos' version of his own plan and words. He had never heard Carlos lose his cool and use the F and MF words that the 'thinking before yapping' Basque said was only spoken by those who had lost control of the situation or themselves.

"Yes, we are fucking about to meet someone who might know where they fucking are!" Carlos added. "And recruit them into OUR cause! If you are fucking alright with that!"

"We're meeting who then?" Vinny inquired in the calm voice and mannerisms that had been, three insults ago, Carlos' domain and trademark.

"A high-level Fascist deserter," Carlos replied, his passion again reined in by reason. After a mind-stabilizing deep breath, he looked around him into the woods.

"Who has been looked after by spirit guides or powerful animal messengers? That's the only way I know that he could have survived being shot, hung, and castrated...before getting killed," continued the pragmatic, above all else, Basque, who believed that beings in the world we can't see are more powerful than those we can. He opened his oversized brown so wide that the fire coming in set fire to the brain's eyes. The source of that fire this time was something in the thick, windblown woods to his left flank.

This time, Vinny's religiously anti-spirit helper eyes saw what Carlos and the two started horses did.

From a distance, it looked like an injured Bigfoot, torn bits of its hide flying in the wind as it stumbled, then crawled its way closer. As it did so, the hide looked more like a medieval woman's frock. Above its blood-stained neck was a short, straggly beard on a very male face. As he pushed his head forward, bending through the last layer of low-lying brush, a bald spot on the crown of his head reflected by the sun blinded Vincent for a moment. When the beast proceeded to the shade, Vinny noticed an unidentifiable military uniform under his frock, along with a depth of humanity in his sorrowful face and a yellow jaundice in the white of his eyes.

"Do you have any water?" the man asked Vincent with a hoarse voice more animal than human, an empty canteen in his shivering hand.

"Do you have a name?" Carlos replied, holding back Vincent's hand from throwing the old, broken, and most probably militarily harmless man his leather pouch of water.

"You do have a name, don't you?" the Basque Captain requested, demanding an answer at the point of his Soviet-made rifle.

The man-beast answered by throwing aside the frock. He pointed to a dog tag hung around the left side of his dirt-caked military tunic. Upon closer examination of the tunic, it was a 20-year-old US Army issue, with one and a half German lapels attached; on his chest were remnants of at least 10 medals. On his forearms were faded cloth in the shape of what had been Sargent stripes.

"I'm Schmitt, more recently anyway," he pushed out of his parched throat with a sense of irony and guilt.

"Or maybe Smith, one of the German-American Bund shitheads from the KKK community of Flathead, Nebraska, who went back to the Old Country for a visit and got drafted by 'accident' into Hitler's Army, right?" Vincent demanded to know, having recognized his very American-accented Spanish, speaking to him in his native tongue. The Italian American wiseguy-crusader whipped out his revolver from his holster, aiming the business end at the lost veteran's head. "Who won those metals and stripes that were torn off that uniform when you were fighting for who, and where!?"

"Who will give us a clearer and more understandable answer if we give him this," Carlos informed Vincent, taking his Comrade's canteen off the saddle horn and throwing it to the old man.

After drowning his thirst and gaining composure, the old black and blue, as well as scar-bearing soldier, treated himself to three deep, more life-sustaining breaths. He then stood up as tall as his aching and shaking legs allowed. "Do you have any food?" he asked, pointing to his grumbling stomach.

"An explanation of where you got those medals, then food, 'Johann Schmitt!'" Vincent barked out.

"It's Wendell Smith," the old man declared proudly. "Once, Sergeant, US Army, after we pushed held the line in the Arden," he said, pointing to discolored portions of his shoulder where there had been Sergeant Major stripes. "And I met someone who, well, made me not want to go home, then unable to. Then...." He broke into mad laughter.

The old veteran of an untold number of wars commenced telling his story with alternating mixtures of a hero's tall tales around a campfire, the desperation of a confessor with a priest, and the relief of a convicted criminal about to allocate to crimes that would put him in the big house for ten years rather than the electric chair for a sizzling ten minutes, he went on. "After pushing the Bolsheviks out of Poland in the Expeditionary Force, I was 'promoted' to Lieutenant Smith, just as the War against the Kaiser was scheduled to end. Then…after getting captured by the Reds and seeing that they were better than the Whites, who wanted to be ruled by the Czar or any other American-funded Imperialist shithead, I got released and then promoted to Comrade Captain Smith. Who well…got stuck in Russia, then assigned to duty in Ukraine in 1930 during the Holodomor, where I…well." Smith slipped into a sorrow based on guilt, the kind that could not be redeemed by ten life sentences in any Soviet Labor Camp or Hard Labor American prison.

"Shit happens. Then after I heard about how Nazi German would put an end to Comrade Stalin's nightmare…." He looked up at Carlos. "You are Carlos, right? I hope you are anyway."

"And you are…THE Wendell Smith," Vincent said, holstering his revolver and his judgment. He recalled the conversations about the past with John Smith that made the present bearable. "With a too good and wise for his own good son named John? And a cool to be cruel other son named 'Orville?'"

"Guilty as charged, to both counts," the ex-Soviet Captain, then American German officer and now a prisoner on the run from his pasts with all sides of the war confessed and related. He took in another breath and looked to the ground, the sky, the horses, then his new 'liberators.' Then, with a blank stare, he looked into himself. "But I didn't kill those Ukrainians who I was assigned to eliminate!" Wendell said. "Our orders from Comrade Stalin were to let them starve to death or accept the realization that they could eat if they became obedient Communist RUSSIAN citizens. Giving up their land. Their families. A third of those poor bastards died of starvation, and a third went to education camps in Siberia. And a third…somehow survived. Determined to side with anyone who would put Stalin in his place and send him to hell, the existence of which he denied, of course. To fight with anyone who opposed Stalin, who is controlling you right now, and you don't even know it!"

"So, you joined the Fascists here in Spain two years ago?" Carlos surmised.

"And left your family back home with no news about where you were and a false story about you dying as a hero. Fighting for your country. For democracy," Vincent shot at the already wounded soul who needed to pay more for his life mistakes and miscalculations.

"A democracy that wouldn't let me be with someone special," Wendell asserted, with more bravery than Vincent saw in any Comrade in the field.

"And that someone else is?" Carlos demanded to know.

"Someone who I will tell you about after I get guarantees of her safety."

"Or his safety?" the homophobic Italian-American inquired.

Wendell replied with three intense beats of silence. "I help you, you help me," Wendell said as his final word on the matter. "Under one condition."

"That your expression of love is kept secret," Carlos said, with more tolerance and perhaps personal experience than Vincent was comfortable with. "There is no law against loving anyone for the right reasons in

Spain that I am fighting for. Or that Comrade Lenin envisioned."

"I'll help you with information or anything else except being recognized by my son, John. If my son John gets sent home before he becomes what I am, or what you both have turned into, in other ways, Carlos and Vincenzo," Wendell demanded. "Deal?" he said, outstretched hand extended to whoever would shake it first.

Carlos, then (under his commander's request) Vincent shook Wendell's hand out of necessity. Each knew that such would probably lead to perhaps more false promises to Wendell Smith made out of necessity. As for Vinny's perspective, he wondered why Wendell Smith-Schmidt knew his name and whereabouts. One possibility was that it was the pictures taken at Beiritz by the celebrity novelist reporter from New York or those snapped by his assistant when he visited the Republican camps. Filled in by perhaps something the freelance journalist put into the article about Vincent in words or between the lines. But Vincent smelled an all too important opportunity occurring with this 'coincidence.'

"You wouldn't know where the DeAngelo family disappeared after they were arrested in Sicily? And where they are now?" he inquired.

"I don't," the ex-captain, and perhaps now Comrade in the service of anyone but Stalin, replied.

"But the man you were supposed to meet a mile down the road could. As long as you…." Wendell slipped into his own world again, emerging from a blank stare with a direct eyeline to Vincent. "He was able to tell you where your 'family' is before he was shot. And as for what they have become…and what became of them? God, if He still exists, knows."

So, I'll make 'him' tell me, Vincent thought but did not say regarding the human informant then the Deity who created him. Instead, he contemplated the price of exacting an accurate definite answer from a 'Being' whose ways of doing things were uncertain and whose intentions were…becoming even more illusive.

CHAPTER 18

Two of the most mature minds in the Abraham Lincoln Brigade belonged to John Smith and Tim Jackson. For the former, it was because of how opened his glistening eyes had been for his nearly forty years of life in places of safety and consistency. For the latter, it was because of what he saw, experienced, and did in the places of change. But the White and Black skinned 'grandpas' found themselves transformed into love-starved and affection-seeking 12-year-old boys in the presence of Jenell, whose special approval they both needed more than they ever imagined.

"What are the eight words in the newly de-segregated Waldorf Astoria dining room I would need to hear from JP Morgan and Henry Ford to know that the Revolution is complete?" Tim Jackson asked Jenell as he brought her a double portion of still hot meat-flavored lentil stew in the 'waiting any day now for an attack' trench atop the hill. "You want potatoes or rice with that steak, Sir?" he delivered with a smile as the punchline.

"And do you know what is the pre-requisite for getting approval for a new, controversial, and highly independent Revolutionary film in Hollywood and Paris?" John proposed to Jenell, bringing her his sliver of freshly baked sugarless jam-topped Happy Birthday Comrade Lenin 'cake' along with two more portions he was able to pilfer from the mess tent. "The group has to approve of it first."

"And what's the best thing you can do for world peace if you're the Jewish head of an elitist, grade triple A art school in Paris or Germany?" Tim delivered to Jenell, pushing his Comrade away from her as subtly as he could.

"If a frustrated, untalented Austrian painter wants into your art school, for God's sake, let him in so he doesn't go into a career in politics," John infused into the offerings from the mortal men to the immortal French goddess.

Jenell knew enough to merely smile at both attempts at humor. She seemed to know that if she let go with a laugh, it would be measured with different yardsticks in Tim and John's minds. "Thank you," she replied to both of them. "For the food for the body," she said to John. "And for the food for the mind," she related to Tim, after which she took one bite of the stew, then another of the 'cake,' then alternating between both entrees as she turned her back on both of them, working her way out of hearing range.

"So…she likes my body more than yours," John said to Tim, feeding his empty stomach on the smile she had given him.

"She relates to my mind!" Tim shot back at John. "And she's an intelligent woman, who just after the FIRST World War…."

"…Decided it was best for both of you to go on separate paths, Comrade Tim?"

"And now decided that we could be on the same one again, John BOY!"

"She danced with me five times last night," John pointed out. "The slow dances."

"Because she knew your white bread legs couldn't handle the fast ones, where your feet actually lift off the floor." Tim pointed out. "It was me she laughed with."

"And me, who she smiled to," John countered.

It went on like that for ten more accusations, insults, and digs, with whispers that drew the two Comrades into yet another war between themselves, such being the major pastime and flaw with anyone on the Left. The banter pulled Jennell into their sphere again.

"Shhh!" she blasted at both of them, after which she stared pensively into the clouds coming in from the North.

"How many planes?" John asked the woman whose ears were as sensitive as the bombs dropped and was loud as he moved the potentially anti-aircraft machine guns into position.

"And what kind?" Tim inquired.

"The kind we need bigger guns for," her reply as she flipped aside her waist-long, ragged mane of unwashed, and not too lice-infested, flaming red hair. "That will drop below those clouds in…."

Upon hearing something no one else could, the French revolutionary who looked and somehow smelled like a freshly clothed and bathed goddess no matter how many layers of sweat and grime coated her size-perfect body by any racial standards continued, flashed her ten-blister coated but somehow manicured fingers five times. Then she turned to the hill to the South. It was covered with a mixture of somehow still-standing brush and sticks of burnt wood that had recently been an olive and cherry orchard. She then flashed all of her fingers four times.

Tim gave the command to the line of Comrades on the left flank to prepare to fire to the North. John ordered the troops in the trench to the right to ready themselves to prepare for a ground attack to come in from the other side.

The attack came from both sides on schedule. But when Tim and John looked between them for the woman they were now dedicated to protecting with as much determination as the protection of the Republic and its Democratic Socialist ideals—Jenell was gone.

The Brains over Balls is an academic Revolutionary from Whitebread Midwest, and the Balls over Brains, grandson of Carolina slaves, focused on fighting the Fascists. In part because their fellow penis-bearing subordinates needed to be inspired. And, to be honest, because the women, or more accurately, woman, was watching…wherever she was.

CHAPTER 19

Sally had fallen into the habit of not looking at the faces of the patients who required her services to put together what bullets and bombs had torn apart. It was a necessary habit which, paradoxically, put more brains into her overworked fingers and lowered the sleep required for her aching but still determined to do the right thing, somehow, head. That cranial vault was concerned of late with matters of the war, and most particularly her husband Jack's involvement in it. Particularly on a week when twice a day, supply trucks reached the hospital with powdered medication that contained no 'accidentally present' toxic material. Along with it was poison-free food. Also, there was a badly needed suture that, unlike previous shipments, didn't break half a day after it was used to sew together severed arteries, intestines, tendons, and nerves. Indeed, 'Gentleman Jack,' as he preferred to be called now, was now one the largest suppliers of legal and illegally obtained supplies for the Republican Cause.

On this day, three new American-made trucks, with tires containing actual treads and motors that had functional mufflers and engines that ran on all cylinders, came into the camp.

"But, is Jack giving equal supply to the other side of the war?" Sally said to herself as she ripped off her (this time in abundance) surgical gloves and mask after reconnecting an arm to a patient who her medical colleague, best friend, and officially, anyway, medical boss, deemed unsavable. "There's no other explanation for a Commie hating, card-carrying Ku Klux Klan member and rising quickly up the ranks G-man giving the Right side of this war so many freebies. War is good business for the 'officially neutral' Capitalists as long as both sides keep fighting. Just like in the last 'Great War,'" she whispered to whatever angels or demons around her were listening.

"Something wrong, Sally?" came without warning from Comrade in all the functional and important ways Juan Fernandez. There was a trusting goodness in his eyes that made her even more reluctant to be around him.

"Everything, and maybe nothing's wrong," Sally replied, assessing her inner and outer inventory, along with her husband's real motives. "Gentleman Jack comes from a comfortable place at home, and he's seen how uncomfortable this war is for we Republicans. And he has seen the faces of the orphans, widows, and widowers who we take care of. And liberate from the freedom-hating Fascists. And as an American, I suppose that his definition of freedom has…hmmm."

"Expanded?" Fernandez suggested. He drew Sally's attention to a portly man with a red suit, big white beard, and white brimmed red hat bearing a red star leaping out of the lead truck as the tarp was flung open by American soldiers in American Army uniforms.

"Merry early Christmas!" 'Santa' boldly declared with exuberance to the civilian refugees who had lost their homes and to the recovering soldiers who had lost their innocence and/or body parts. They gathered around the bearded 'elves' Santa brought with him, distributing gustatory delights beyond stale bread and lentils. Along with new clothing for the upcoming winter. And a mixture of portable musical instruments that found their way almost instantly into the hands of those who could play them.

"And Santa Jack has a special gift for you, Miss Sally," Juan Fernandez said with a courtly bow as he handed, to his knowledge anyway, an unmarried wonder woman a gift-wrapped book. She grabbed it away from Fernandez, put on surgical gloves and a smock, then opened the gift carefully.

"A Christmas Carol," Juan noted, reading the title of the book. The 'Merry Christmas' greeting inside of it was addressed to Sally by the man who was, legally anyway, her husband. "A tale about a miserly asshole who turned into a generous saint after assessing his past, present and possible future," he recalled and gave voice to, "Which, as we all know, happens a lot here." His gaze turned inward, averting his eyes and thoughts.

"Yeah, maybe you're right," Sally conceded, her lips breaking into a smile. Somehow, she forgot all of the misery and setbacks she had inadvertently caused the Republic by not revealing 'Gentleman Jack's' history as a commie-hating G-man back home. A man who had perpetrated the Red Scare in the service of so many who got rich and comfortable. At the expense of Jews, Negroes, and Catholic immigrants, of course, who, after all, were accustomed to being 'uncomfortable.' And, of course, non-WASPs who should, for their own good, 'know and keep to' their place in the American hierarchy.

An impromptu band of refugees, patients, and staff broke into a Spanish song conducted by Santa himself. That plethora of abruptly hopeful souls who could walk or hobble converted the frozen solid early morning ground into a dance floor. Men danced with women, women with women. And even a few men with men!

"May I?" Juan asked Sally, opening up his arms.

"Sure," Sally conceded. She found her feet taking to the dance floor with a slow movement that made her feel muscles in her legs she had ignored. And a lightness in her heart that escalated as Juan picked up the pace and her spirits. She felt breath in her lungs rather than dusty air. Hope for a future. She was turning into someone who wanted to remain above ground rather than having to. Her smile turned into a laugh as she lost herself in Juan's eyes and heart. After which, he did a swirl, found herself, and passed on to a Polish patient she had saved from self-imposed as well as Fascist bullets. The dance continued, which rotated her eyes to see a bruised face and then an injured body connected to it peering out of a partially open flap of the third, still unopened, truck.

"Ilene!" Sally gasped, her eyes meeting her stepdaughter she left behind so she could save more daughters.

"I fell down the stairs," Ilene mouthed to Sally, who now was not thankful that she could read lips or eyes.

Sally did her best to excuse herself from the Polish patient's dancing, but he held on to her. "Enjoy the moment; it is a needed medicine for the doctor," he said as he gripped her even harder with each attempt she made to get to her injured and, upon further examination, chained-up stepdaughter. "You saved me from dying; I give you life. Good trade?"

Sally looked at Santa Jack, who gazed back, threatening at her. "One more small favor, and Ilene's all yours," he mouthed with lips that still retained a smile the crowd bought as generous. "A small favor, pour favor, for everyone."

"I must go now," Sally said to the Pole, who had been her greatest 'miracle case' in the OR, in Russian, and then Spanish.

"After we finish the dance," he insisted, in very American English, trapping her into a dance in his strong arms, made functional by her efforts to save a life she thought worth saving. "Your husband cares about you both, who he loves, and the world," was his final words.

Sally, being a pragmatic masochist who still lapsed into believing in universal goodness, tortured herself with another look at her husband. He, indeed, was very good at appearing to be sincere and caring. But for what purpose? She pondered what kind of 'love' would have made a man be so vicious to his own daughter, his own countrymen, and his own fellow citizens of the world. But what was he now? What was his real agenda and reason for schlepping across the pond and into a country that was difficult to get into without papers and even more difficult to get out of alive? It wasn't the first time, and or the last, that Sally, an excellent reader of minds, had misread hearts.

CHAPTER 20

This time, the mission was simple, as related to Comrade Lt. Vinny DeAngelo and demoted to the same rank as Comrade Carlos Garcia. Follow the trucks bringing the Republican prisoners taken by Fascist forces outside of Burgos and see that they are not exported to Italy or Germany as 'volunteer workers' or corpses. And if they 'come to their senses' and take up arms with Franco's Nationalist forces for the cause of 'stopping the Communist cancer,' they see that they or their families pay the price for that 'education.' Yes, it was a special Mission reserved for Vinny and Carlos. They were one of the best reconnaissance teams on the ground. They could smell out the enemy as well as infiltrate any Fascist camp as a German (in the case of the Berlin-educated Basque) or an Italian advisor. Or maybe this mission was punishment for them being the only Republicans whose dumb luck left them standing on their own two feet without chains around them after a squirmish ten days ago with Nationalist forces that decimated everyone else around them.

This time DeAngelo, in an Italian officer's uniform, and Garcia, sporting a Nazi tunic with a black skull on the lapel, was issued a different kind of horse than in previous missions to be used in the high country above the valley roads taken by covered Fascist trucks.

"Two wheels beats four legs anytime," confident ace motorcyclist Vinny said to Carlos as the latter, behind him, nearly lost his balance on the captured motorcycles converted into sturdy dirt bikes. They were sure-footed beasts on the twisted paths through the high country woods overlooking the roads on the treeless valley below, being fed by a gentle rain. Meanwhile, the high country wind blew into his face, pushing Vincent's overgrown black mane back so hard that he could feel it at its roots. "We'll be at the Fascist camp before those trucks below us can even see it!"

"As long as there's solid ground ahead of us and not snow," Carlos pointed out as the glaze of frozen hard ground ahead of them gave way to centimeters of slippery snow. As they advanced upward, large flakes of snow fell from the sky. "We can't trot these wheeled beasts through snow and ice."

"So, we gallop through it," Vinny volleyed back. He wiped the layer of fresh snow from his goggles, proceeding forward at full speed. "Like buffalo, who push through a storm blowing into their face and come out on the other side fast instead of cows who turn around, running away from it, rewarded for their 'sensibility' with wet asses and cold balls."

"But...cows don't have balls," Carlos replied as he followed Vinny over what seemed to be the most solid ground available.

"But we do," Vincent yelled back as he headed further up the mountain. Each turn pushed him against the oncoming wind as it challenged it. "And when it comes to what's more important, brains or balls...."

Mother Nature intervened with her comment on the matter in the form of a patch of mud that was coated with ice. Vinny's bike decided that it was not up to the task of staying upright. The front wheel flew off, obeying the law of gravity rather than its 'master's' command. "Mother fucking cock-sucking shit!" Vincent yelled out as he saw the wheel take a ride down the hill and then disappear into an abyss.

Carlos yelled out an expletive in Basque with twice as much frustration and most probably ten times more, four times more vulgarity, as his bike slipped into a sideways slip. It left him with bruised rather than broken bones, so he hoped anyway. When both 'easy riders' looked down the hill, their jaws dropped.

"So, Franco's Nationalist headquarters is closer to our lines than the map said it was," Carlos noted, as quietly as possible, his painful chest pinned to the frozen ground. "And the prisoners, our Comrades, who they took are already there," he said after getting a closer look with Soviet-made field glasses.

"What's left of them," Vincent added, pointing his compadre to an open grave filled with freshly shot bodies. Disarmed witnesses were forced to watch another six comrades sent to join them by a firing squad. "And where's the 'prisoner of interest' we're supposed to get out at any cost?"

Carlos pointed Vincent's attention to another area of the camp as they shared a closer view with the field glasses as well as shared perspectives. A blindfolded man covered with more fresh blood and burns than intact skin was being escorted to an impromptu stage in the middle of the camp. "Viva la Revolution!" the new 'star' of the show slurred out of what was left of his mouth, louder with each whipping of his back. He was pulled up onto the platform in front of the other prisoners, all of whom saluted him in Republican style. One of the prisoners began to sing the Internationale and was joined in by everyone else till they were silenced with machine gun fire in front of their bare feet and, for some, into their feet. A Spanish Nationalist Sargent chained the 'star' prisoner's left arm to one post, a smaller framed corporal securing what was left of his right forelimb to another post. A proud private with the face of a shithead stoked a fire with a white-hot iron rod. Still, when asked to provide the position of the troops he had sent into retreat, the battle plans for the Republican Army, the port where the next Soviet Arms would be coming into, and the names of the Republican spies amongst the Nationalists, the prisoner remained defiantly silent.

"The kind of stand-up guy who won't rat on anyone and won't talk, no matter how much shit they threw on him," Vincent said. "Like my uncle Sal and godfather Joe in Sicily, and father back home in Brooklyn. And, when it comes to it, I hope me."

"Everybody talks," Carlos related and confessed. "Especially when the executioners are commanded by…experts." He referred Vincent's attention to a spit-shined car pulling in. Two Italian Army officers emerged from it. They were led like dignitaries with bows and salutes by the Spanish Nationalists and the resident Spanish priest to the platform. "Experts who are—"

"—Uncle Sal and Godfather…Joe?" Vincent noted, his jaw-dropping in disbelief when he saw their faces. "Who, yeah, are gonna liberate everyone," he boasted with pride.

"Or maybe not," Carlos interjected as Uncle Sal took a hot rod into his gloved hand, and Godfather Joe pointed to the prisoner's left eye.

"If thine eyes see evil, pluck them out!" the priest behind him proclaimed, after which Sal burnt a hole into the star prisoner's ocular porthole, leaving a black tunnel in its wake. "Confess," the priest commanded the uni-eyed prisoner. "Tell us what we need to know to eradicate the Communist Cancer."

"Which means where your supply lines are, who your allies are, and what their battle plans are," Uncle Sal blasted into the prisoner's still-not-screaming face.

"And where your family lives, so we can send them your body, comrade Colonel. If you tell us what we need to know, your family will be spared what everyone else's family here will get and deserve," Godfather Joe growled toward his remaining right eye. "Or else we will have to—you know, we'll have to burn another hole into your thick head," Godfather Joe continued. "Or you can tell us what you know, and you and your men can live another day. And fight with, instead of against us."

The prisoner's will weakened. He seemed to be thinking about the proposition. "You do know what we have to do," Godfather Joe added with the superiority of a man who was king over not only his subjects but the moral code he chose for them.

"And what has to be done," Uncle Sal added, smirking with sadistic delight as he moved the hot iron toward the prisoner's remaining eye.

"Yes, we know, Comrade Colonel Emilo, what has to be done," Vinny, the shocked and now angered Italian-American, heard from Carlos, addressing and finally naming the 'special prisoner.' He retrieved a long-range rifle with a silencer from the motorcycle and tossed another one to Vincent. Without missing a beat in the symphony or necessary horrors, Carlos took aim and shot the Comrade hero Colonel in the head, ending his misery and, perhaps, compromises with reality. "He was my brother," Carlos said by way of explanation. "And now you—"

In the three seconds of contemplation available, Vincent took aim through the power sites at Uncle Sal and Godfather Joe. The men who he thought were heroes who defied Mussolini but who, out of cowardice or monetary advantage, decided to join forces with the 'Law and Order' promising and cruelty-delivering dictator. Two seconds and three shots later, Joe and Sal were sent to their just reward. They fell into the arms of the priest, who threw them aside as if they were slain demons who would take him to hell.

"And now you," Vincent grunted. He ended the priest's service to the God who the Fascists had bought favor with courtesy by delivering another two shots. The first at his testicles. The second into his cold heart. "Maybe it was, or maybe it wasn't the 'good father' who took away my and my brother's childhood…but…he's from the same fucking fucked up tribe," the Italian American Wiseguy, who flirted with women but never could somehow consummate a relationship with any of them, said to Carlos.

"Yes, I do know," Carlos replied. He hugged Vincent close enough not to trap him in the kind of relationship no one wanted. But close enough for the once life-loving man who was now converted into a walking corpse to consider that living was a better choice than intentionally dying.

As for the rest of the mission, the Spanish Nationalist troops felt cursed by the unseen gods who fired shots from the sky at their leaders. While they were looking upward, the remaining prisoners stormed them, taking over the camp and taking back their dignity. Mission accomplished, with a victorious ending. For those on the ground below the mountain overlook anyway.

CHAPTER 21

Logic said that after the historically unprecedented carpet bombing of Guernica, which killed more civilians than Republican soldiers, world support for the Republican cause would shoot up like a limber cat fleeing up a tree while chased by a rabid dog. But the War was going even worse for the anti-Fascist forces. The Northern and Southern belts of Republican territories were shrinking as fast as the rations of food, medicine, and ammunition. And as the 50% of the foreign volunteers still functionally alive knew all too well, 'singing' bullets or enlightenment across no man's land into Franco's fuckheads didn't work. Still, some Republicans chose to use music as a way to strengthen themselves and weaken the will of the enemy.

In his last hand-written will, Scottish Socialist Angus McFee left his great grandfather's Jacobi saber to Tim Jackson as long as he promised to polish it with Fascist blood. McFee bequeathed his kilt to Jenell on the condition that she shave her French legs once every fortnight. And his bagpipes to John Smith since the 'still stuck in Sunday church services' WASP Midwesterner had as much talent to play it as his legs were made for dancing. But McFee somehow saw an expressive artist inside the ultra-reserved Bible-belt-raised academic who would someday 'learn how to shake a wicked hoof' with the right woman on the dance floor and serenade his way to the alter with her with a bagpipe love song.

John's attempt to play the bagpipes was amplified by his thinking he hit more of the right notes than he actually did. "Are you sure that this is supposed to scare the Fascists away from their trenches?" a newly arrived private said to Comrade Captain Tim while waiting for yet another battle with the enemy in the second month of a stalemate between trenches.

"It will hurt their ears and prevent them from hearing any of us who are trying to sneak up on them," Jenell explained.

"And what about us?" the private yelled at the most attractive and brave woman in the company as the lad placed his hands over his elephant-sized auditory appendages.

"We use hand signals," she said with wide-open lips appended by flowing movements of her fingers in a sort of sign language she had taught everyone around her. "And learn how to read lips. Like when the fat lady sings too loudly on stage, or the audience or the police are trying to boo you out of the concert hall because you're playing the politically incorrect symphony," she yelled into the Private's aching ears. She handed the peach fuzz-faced private who had given up his post as an aspiring music conductor at the Rochester School of Music to put his theories about Revolutionary Politics into practice an additional ration of cotton balls for his ears.

Meanwhile, John blew every ounce of passion in his parched lungs into the bagpipes, running back and forth in the trench so that the squawks of that most traditional and frightening of instruments would seem to be echoing on every side of the valley. A valley which, by European standards anyway, was a rock canyon.

"Sincerity," Jenell said, mouthed and 'finger talked' to Tim with a warm smile regarding John's newly found passion for being a practitioner of the arts. "Maybe it is more contagious than depression, lifelessness of spirit, or cruelty."

"He still has a wife," Tim reminded her.

"So did you when we met," Jenell reminded the veteran. "But here in Europe, we know that you can't get all the groceries your heart needs at the same store."

"Like you're doing, Jenell, with me and John?" Tim realized in the passion of the moment, forced by the possibility of death, yet again, the necessity to not die without stating the truth to someone who needed to know it.

Jenell answered yet again with an even bigger smile, then a kiss on Tim's parched lips. Tim felt it as being a 'yes' in a way that still allowed Comrades to remain Comrades, with terms of endearment that were both eternal and ever-evolving. Losing then finding himself in her eyes, it felt like one of those 'Eternal Now' moments which always was, always is and always will be. Just in time for the FASCIST commander in the opposing trench to request that the music stop.

Such was answered with gunfire from the Republican right and left flanks. It unleashed a prelude to yet another battle in this war of attrition, which, maybe, would, yet again, be the last battle to see who got to take over the charred, blown-up valley. Meanwhile, John kept on playing the bagpipes with the dedication of a standard bearer in times of old. Yes, it would be a victorious day for the Republicans, no matter what the outcome. Unless, of course, the Irish Blue shirts fighting to keep the Fascists in charge of the government houses and the Catholic Priests in control of even the Atheists' souls had brought with them their own bagpipes or tubas.

CHAPTER 22

Sally's special needs 'accident prone' stepdaughter Ilene was safely away from the fighting. But she was experiencing advancing puberty, her second menstruation, and the crushes she was developing on the young men assigned to keep her safe, fed, and entertained. Sally's husband, G Man Jack, had given up 'requesting' Sally to curtail her activities to serve the Democratic Socialist Revolution so that Ilene would not experience more 'unnecessary hardships' at her biological father's hands.

Sally now felt…relieved. The self-taught super-woman who was good at everything she took on, except being kind to herself, continued to do what she could for the Republican cause, but mostly as a doctor and not a combatant. When not saving lives on makeshift operating tables, she actively trained new recruits on how to take the lives of Franco's troops on the battlefield. But she needed to be more direct in her War against the Fascists. She was angered beyond measure at being assigned by her Comrade Boss, Fernandez, to remain available for 'special assignments' in the back lines.

"There's an American expression, those who can't do teach," Sally protested to now full Colonel Juan Fernandez, yet again, as a jeep came into camp. It was to transport her to her next location, well behind the lines, her most personal belongings being packed in it for her as a courtesy. "It stands to reason that I can be very effective on the front lines killing Fascists. Consider it on-the-job training I'd do WITH the new replacements!" she protested.

"Yes, I know, but there is a chain of command here, Sally," Juan replied as yet another friend who was protecting Sally from herself. And the truth of what was going on around her.

"With you promoted to full Colonel, Juan," she pointed out, seductively swooning in toward his rigidly postured chest, sneaking her finger under his shirt. But before she could caress the special spots which, due to his male biology, would weaken Juan's resolve, he gently pushed her arm away. He tenderly held onto her wrist, which was connected to a tightly clenched fist.

"I was promoted to full Colonel because every one of my commanders led from the front and didn't come back to camp after the battle was over!" he barked back at Sally. After which, he let go of her wrist, his eyes facing inward yet again. "Or if they did return after leading men from the front, it was without arms, legs, eyes or…a functional brain to process anything due to the kinds of wounds you can't see."

Sally pulled back her assault, allowing Juan to process and maybe even heal the wounds that none of her magic potions or surgical prowess could fix. "You think I'm so important to the cause. So let me really BE more important to the cause! OUR cause!" she countered, hugging him from behind with all of her might. "And," she continued, seeing the rest of her personal belongings being put on the jeep. "Why are you sending me away from the man I want to die with and for?" she self-observed herself saying.

"Because your presence was requested and is needed by someone more powerful than me," Juan directed as kindly as he could into Sally's face. He offered her an envelope with a faded ornate Spanish seal. "And it's not 'Gentleman' Jack Whitaker, who, well, I know you know better than you told me. He has left Spain, and he left this for you." He pulled out another envelope bearing the emblem of an American Monastery for the rich and repentant in Vermont as a return address.

"I always liked to eat my ice cream, as I remember it anyway, before the broccoli. Or the lentil soup before the stale bread," she mused, reaching for the more ornate envelope first. "The Presidential Spanish

Republican Seal," she noted while opening it. "Ever notice that the most broke, poorest, and least stable countries have the most ornate artwork on their coat of arms and flags? Even Democratic Socialist countries like…." Her jaw dropped upon reading the contents of the offer she was not allowed to refuse.

"President Comrade Doctor Juan Negrin," Juan said. "A brilliant researcher who became a brilliant doctor than a brilliant teacher then, all things considered —"

"—A brilliant, all things considered, President," Sally interjected, putting aside that Juan may have read the letter addressed to her already. Or that she had insight into the man who sent it. "Your President wants to give me a medal?"

"And a promotion to…maybe being my boss?" Juan smiled back. "Queen Elizabeth, the First, was a better ruler of England than most of the men who plopped sat their asses on that throne."

Because she didn't get involved with men, officially anyway, Sally pondered but didn't say. "But, what about that other letter?" she asked, taking the plain Jane American envelope from her now out-of-country husband with numerous stamps on it into her trembling hand. "Which says…?"

"Something I know nothing about and won't ask you about either, Sally," Juan replied,

Sally imagined what G-Man Jack Whittaker would look like in a scratchy burlap monk's robe rather than the hundred-dollar three-piece grey suits he wore year-round. Suits he cleaned every time he stained it with Sally's blood when she got political. Or the sanguineous fluid from his daughter Ilene when she got 'difficult.' She chuckled. Then she wondered if her generously follicled husband would actually consent to having the crown of his head shaved in a monk's circle. So, as the residents of the Lord's Redemption Monastery claimed, they could 'more clearly receive the messages into their thick skulls from the Heavenly Father above.'

Sally felt her heart open to the possibility that 'what goes around comes around' works for those who did good deeds as well as bad ones. And allowed herself to provisionally believe that being a good person around a bad one DOES result in the contagion of 'GOODNESS' to infect and cure evil souls. She finally opened the letter.

"Our socialist President has betrayed the Revolution,

Dearest Sally. I ask you to find out what his secrets are and what really happened to the money the people entrusted to him. Tell me, and I will see that our American government puts someone else in his position who is worthy of it. Maybe even you? Do this, and Ilene is yours. She has always been more yours than mine anyway, which is maybe why I was so cruel to both of you. In the meantime, I beg your forgiveness and forgiveness for so many things I have done wrong. The doctors here say it was because of a brain tumor I have had for so many years that gives me headaches now. That…maybe you can take out because you become the skilled doctor that you are, despite everything I did for and to you? With love that I tragically expressed as hate for you and so many others, Brother Jack."

Sally took in a deep breath. She felt the dry, cold air erupting up and down her spine, as she considered what was ahead and said goodbye to what was behind. Indeed, as in Revolutionary Blues, the metaphysical novel about the Yaqui Indian revolution in Mexico she had written, man, in the service of humanity, had de-possessed the devil. Four, or perhaps forty, internal revelations later, measured as ten seconds in 'real' time, and daydreaming the plotline for the sequel of the unpublished novel, she was awakened by a honking horn.

"A new life awaits you, Comrade," Juan said with a smile almost as big as hers. "And new Life for the Revolution! A people's revolution of body, mind, and spirit that—"

Sally silenced Juan's politically blissful rant with a tight kiss and plummeted under the recesses of his overgrown 'bigger than even Comrade Stalin's' mustache, feeling him and her to be the same soul. Both hearts had experienced the thaw of a long winter, smelling the aroma of fresh flowers underneath the ice coating their secret-holding souls. Flowers that, hopefully, would not give any of them hay fever.

CHAPTER 23

Sally's experience with award ceremonies in Spain was far different than what she expected. The pinning of a medal or higher rank insignia on foreigners who had just come back from saving Republican lives or ending Fascist ones contained a mixture of aristocratic formalities and was accompanied by all military groups. Such also contained humor-infused 'way to go Comrade' improvised comments by the awarder, with similar, often expletive-containing, retorts by the awardee. They were followed, of course, by officers and enlisted men getting equally drunk afterward to the tune of yet another song that would not be a hit anywhere in America except in Socialist meeting halls. The placing of medals on the chests of the freedom fighters whose souls had left their bodies or which were awarded to the families they left behind was a matter of a more 'metaphysical' austerity, of course, with music that was more somber.

The pictures Sally had seen of Republican President Juan Negrin, with a naturally fat face and 'boss man' eyes, made him seem to be more like an overly fed Al Capone rather than a leader of a Cause running out of food, medicine, and ammunition. But for reasons she did not understand, Hispanic leaders did seem to need to appear well-fed to be attractive to women and inspiring to their followers. He laid the Lauriete Plate of Madrid around Sally's bowed neck in front of a tavern in a town she had never heard of, which was, for today anyway, the Presidential Palace. Sally lifted her head in anticipation of hearing a song with a mixture of hope, sorrow, and defiance. But there were no musicians amongst the line of Army Officers and Civilian officials. Just applause, given with smiles when deliverers of such looked at Sally. And grimaces of displeasure when at least half of them gazed towards Negrin.

"If you're popular with everyone, it means you aren't doing your job," Sally whispered into the ear of the worn-out, life-tired President when he hugged her, revealing that his suit was now two sizes too large for his slender, grumbling belly. "And, if you want to, you can lower your hands below my waist," she continued to the forty-six going-on-the sixty-four-year-old official leader of the 'leaderless' Revolutionary Republic. "As long as I can slap you on your ass also," she continued to the man who took on leadership of the Cause just as it was being challenged most.

Negrin's chuckling smile broke through his overgrown mustache. The wrinkles on his face seemed to recede into a mug that, as Sally experienced it, was still as youthful and hopeful as it was before this war against oppression and against war itself had begun.

Sally allowed the edge of her lips to pull upward. She gazed at and into Negrin's not-so-baby brown eyes. Indeed, there was a plethora of thoughts brewing behind them. But she couldn't define which they were. Was there a lost child behind them, a hurting man, or just another political animal who knew that the law of the jungle was to eat or be eaten? With as much effort as she could, Sally opened up her mind to all ideas possible, allowing each of those speculations to link with all of the others. But before any connections could be made, she was interrupted by politics.

"Comrade President," she heard from a General as he looked at his watch. "We have to move on."

"Yes, as do I," Negrin replied, looking at and into Sally. "I will see all of you in my office, assuming it isn't bombed out or taken over by rats again in two hours," he told his underlings as he turned to them.

"One hour would be better, Comrade Juan," said a short, thin civilian official, the only one of the dozen 'assistant Comrades' who seemed to care about the President as a man.

"An hour and a half, then?" Negrin proposed.

The men looked at each other, conferring their thoughts without a spoken word, then conveyed the vote to the General. "An hour and a half then," the General said with the upturned chin of an aristocratic power monger Duke about to extract exactly what he wanted from the king he was pledged to serve. He marched away, his riding crop in hand, tapping it on his polished boots, signaling the rest of the Officers and then the Ministers to follow.

"Yes, sometimes the means do not justify the ends," Negrin related and confessed to Sally with a trusting tone. One which, Sally hoped, would remain active and honest. She, of course, for the sake of all the right causes, kept her real agenda for coming here to accept his hospitality. "If you wish to, I would like to make you an offer you can't refuse. Or, if I know you as I think I do, won't refuse, Professor, possibly one day, President Doctor Comrade Sally?" He opened the door to a car that had been decorated with bullet holes, inviting her to go in.

It was the Professor who tilted the needle to accept the invitation rather than being the first female leader of a Democratic Socialist country. Despite the fact that women did have the right to vote in Republican Spain, they didn't seem to be taking full advantage of it…yet.

Negrin chose to drive the car himself, speaking not a word to Sally en route to the destination. Finally, after passing through three destroyed villages and as many which were being slowly rebuilt, they reached a charred but still proudly standing two-story brick building. The first story was halfway underground, with curtains covering every window. It was supplied with electricity from a generator bigger than any Sally had seen, along with no less than five Tesla coils. It was protected by guards who spoke no Spanish or English, at least when Sally asked about the name of the building, which reminded her of the biomedical training she got in New England. Such was before, of course, she was 'dismissed' from the university for being more interested in political science than industrial or medical science.

Finally, after Sally had futilely tried to start a conversation with the six guards in as many languages, Nergin, having dealt with a few reports waiting for him at the mailbox, approached her. "So, you have one key question you want to ask me," he said. "Which I will answer honestly."

It wasn't the first time Sally had heard a politician claim to answer a question honestly, which, of course, meant that you were going to be told at least part of the truth. In search of such a fraction of reality, she put her hand over her mouth in a professorial manner, looked up to the sky as if to be negotiating with the gods or God "herself," and then stared at the medal around her neck. "There are many other Republican serving men and women who were more brilliant doctors than I am," she put forth. "And who actually went into combat rather than being assigned constantly to stay in the back lines to treat the wounded." Boldly, she looked into President Negrin's eyes. "So, why did you award this medal to me?" she demanded to know. "And why did you bring me here to this…isolated 'facility?'"

Negrin pulled his lips back into a smile of gratitude. He then pulled out three pictures from his breast pocket overlying his heart. "My two sons and wife got very, very sick when they were exposed to a poisonous white powder that smelled like peppermint, which was delivered by a traitor who put it into my son's birthday cake. I didn't get a chance to taste it because I was, well…serving the people elsewhere and not my family at home."

As Negrin described the conditions that tore apart his family's lungs and other vital organs, Sally's jaw dropped. And when Negrin went on about how the traitor denied having any knowledge of the toxic nature of the special spice up to the time of his necessary execution, Sally envisioned the same punishment for her due to knowing about the toxic powder distributed, most probably by her husband. Perhaps to both sides of this War until he decided, for reasons she could not figure out, to support the Republicans. A toxic powder that had a cure, which he told Sally about, and no one else, a long time ago when he had used it to 'depopulate undesirable populations' in Latin-American countries who didn't value being taken over by American industrialists.

"But," Negrin related after his angry and sorrowful rant about what the toxin did to his family and others. "It was this that saved them." He pulled out folded papers from his pants pocket with formula sheets detailing how to manufacture and administer an antidote and vaccine against the unnamed toxin. "You didn't sign it, but when I saw your reports from the battlefield about other cures for diseases and treatments for injuries which were not in any textbook I read, all of which worked, I recognized the handwriting and finally found the author! It was YOU who saved so many people from the North American toxin that found its way to Spain."

"Who was not trying to create a disease with a cure that would be sold to the highest bidder, or obedient populations…or…like the Fascists in the American government are capable of doing in the cause of keeping power or getting rich," Sally self observed herself asserting. She voiced the agenda that no doubt her husband, FBI Agent Jack Whittaker, had upon his arrival in Spain. And his madder than proficient Great Grandfather, 'Doc 'Mirakel' Steiner' had when giving smallpox-infected blankets to freezing Indians while thinking he was going to get rich selling the cure to all of the Reservations and the white communities around them. "Whatever you want or need to do to me, I accept," Sally stated with calm resolve.

"Or do FOR you?" Negrin volleyed back with a bow reeking of admiration and respect. He opened the padlock lock to the bottom floor of the 19th-century brick stronghold with what looked like an 18th-century key. He invited Sally to enter the darkened chamber.

Her first impression of the room was through her nostrils. "Rats and rat shit," she said.

"And rabbits and rabbit raisins," Negrin added, turning on the lights. "And some mice and hamsters, too," he said of the caged animals in the state-of-the-art medical laboratory. "But not Nationalist Fascist prisoners as test subjects," he added. "Though the doctors in Germany and Italy have been experimenting with Communist, Jewish and homosexual prisoners to advance their knowledge of biomedical 'medicine.' Which…well, my advisors say we DO need to fight fire with fire. But…."

"Fascist prisoners are not human; therefore, what works on them won't work on anyone else?" Sally advanced, breaking Negrin's recurring spell of inner reflection. "But we can use them as an experiment model of the neurochemistry of cruelty."

"Or, more accurately, ignorance, which inevitably leads to all cruelty, according to Socrates anyway,"

Negrin assertively suggested as he thumbed through a lab book and administered appropriate medications to rodents in specific cages. His eyes indicated that he indeed felt sorrow for the rats who were living in cages on pellets rather than on the street dining on human corpses. He offered an explanation for what he was about to do with them. "What we learn from experimenting with twenty rats can save two hundred dogs or four hundred horses. Or, though most of them these days don't deserve it, forty thousand American 'neutrals' who…."

"…Can and will become Democratic Socialists when we kick the Fascists out of Spain," Sally proclaimed. "Then kick them out of Italy and Germany," she asserted. "Or…" She gazed at the scientist whose revolutionary research in neuroscience, as well as teaching doctors how to be research scientists before he became President, had made Spanish science world-class to those who would look at it openly anyway. "We can cure the political ills of the world with science instead of using science to find more 'interesting' and money-making ways to destroy humanity. Which…"

Sally's discourse of hope and enthusiasm was interrupted by a chuckle, then a guffaw, then a full-blown belly laugh from Negrin.

"What?" she shouted at him. "What did I say that was so fucking funny!!!?"

"What you said, and how you said it, reminded me of…someone else," Professor Doctor Presidente Negrin pushed out of his mouth between laughs as he recollected his thoughts. With his hand covering his chin in a 'professorial' manner, he surveyed Sally, from her shapely calves visible to the dress bearing the colors of the Republican flag she had been requested to wear for the award ceremony to her ample breasts made to seem larger due to the low cut line of the garment, to her flowing blonde hair which had been styled for the first time since leaving New York, then down again, no less than three times.

"I remind you of someone else," Sally retorted with furled eyebrows. "All of us gals who refuse to look like old maids before our time have a habit of doing that. But…."

"Felicia," he said, with fondness, after which he pulled out a pocketwatch bearing a young woman's picture. "Felecia de Dum Pablo," he continued with respect. "A lab assistant who became my most valued and brilliant pupil," he concluded with a bitter-sweet tone.

"And secret lover?" Sally advanced after allowing Negrin, or rather Juan, a few private moments to relive memories his brain was still processing, which his heart was still stubbornly holding onto. "Who…."

"…You and the newspapers would like to know more about it, no doubt," Juan added.

"The newspapers, not me," Sally replied. "And I don't work for the newspapers, Juan. I mean President…"

"Then who do you work for, Sally?" he requested and demanded.

"The same cause that you did and still do?" she boldly advanced. "Even though…the end justifies the means. The means like—"

"—Ah, yes!" Negrin spouted back. "Like that business of why I transferred seventy percent of the Spanish gold reserves to the Soviet Union before the Nationalists almost overran Madrid a year ago and took it for themselves. Which my opponents and the 'neutrals' say made me a servant of Joseph Stalin. Without Comrade Stalin's help, the Fascists would have taken over my country, my vision, and my people a long time ago! But…that gold…is NOT in Stalin's private vault!" he asserted. He turned his back to Sally, yelling at the sky above the roof of the dusty yet still, according to the stacks of published and yet-to-be-published manuscripts, the productive lab he had been keeping alive. "And the money my allies and enemies say I stole is safe with trusted parties," he continued, placing another piece of paper from his pocket into Sally's shaking hand. "Who have had to take refuge in the Soviet Union, Felicia…I mean, Sally."

"No, you mean Felicia, which is…fine," Sally said. "Who…will not betray your trust," she continued, not sure if she was telling the truth or lying.

"Who will be able to integrate the love of family with a love of and for the people," Negrin asserted.

"Of that, I am sure, Comrade Sally, whatever happens to me or the Revolution," he continued, hugging Sally. "And I thank you for saving the lives of my children."

Sally couldn't help thinking about her own child, Ilene. Though she was Sally's stepdaughter, she meant more to her than any child she could. A stepdaughter whose welfare and destiny had now become Sally's main concern. Perhaps because Sally needed to be a mother or because Ilene could do more for the world than her stepmom ever could.

"We all have, or should have, one child who will and must tell the truth about us to future generations," Negrin said as if his X-ray vision read Sally's mind and soul. Or maybe it was because he had the kind of dumb luck all successful biomedical researchers and clinicians have. "Future generations are in positions to do more than we ever could, now and in the future, as untainted souls. And as we know, or should know, Judas was Jesus' favorite and most trusted disciple. Who did what he was assigned to do for Jesus and all the rest of us."

Sally was familiar with the theory that Greek Visionary writer Nikos Katzanzakis was about to put into a book that would get him excommunicated by the church. But be a welcomed dinner guest with God the Father and Jesus the Son in Heaven or Valhalla. Was this mystery about to enter the real world once again? The answer lay somehow in a notebook Negrin handed her. A pen was attached to its twisted, discolored spiral binding.

"The first half of this I wrote, the second half you will write, after you ask me some more questions which I will over answer, with a painful but necessary honesty," he said. He sent the lab assistants away from the laboratory, invited Sally to sit down on a chair, then plopped his ass on a stool a foot lower than hers.

CHAPTER 24

For reasons he didn't know but knew enough to not too aggressively question, Tim Jackson was removed from duty in the field at the height of his success. He was assigned, by Presidential decree, to pick up and then drive 'a special lady' to the American Consulate in Barcelona. He resented not only the mission but the change in uniform, a plain black suit with a chauffeur's cap.

"Orders are orders," said Carlos from the back seat, clad in a wide-collared white jacket with a red shirt and blue tie in the American-made car bearing the Stars and Stripes as they drove past the last checkpoint in a deserted village. It had burnt to the ground so that the Fascist forces that took it over could dine on nothing but ashes and take out their frustrations on cockroaches rather than farm animals or people.

"Going through our own territory to Barcelona would have been a lot safer, Sir," Jackson barked back from the driver's seat.

"But not faster," Carlos pointed out. "And this mission is—"

"—of utmost importance, yeah, I know," Tim replied. "So what happens if someone decides to make us take off these costumes and they see the Republican tunics under them?"

"We'll be sent to prisoner-of-war camps instead of shot as spies," Carlos answered. "Theoretically, anyway." He noted on the side of the road three 'civilians' with Republican Army trousers and civilian coats being lined against what was left of a wall in front of a firing squad. Carlos flinched when the shots were fired.

"Yeah, so much for intelligence about the enemy," Jackson said to Carlos. "And I hope those trousers you got on are still dry in the crotch."

Carlos hid the evidence that they weren't, then motioned for Jackson to drive on. "It's alright," Jackson replied with an understanding tone. "Courage and bravery are temporary traits that happen to and for us, on their own time. And in the meantime…."

Having inherited the power of song from his slave ancestors, 'Chauffer Tim' broke into a gospel song.

"And before I'll be a slave, I'll be buried in my grave," it began. It sustained Carlos, somehow. He assured veteran black-as-coal former 'Doughboy' Jackson that he wouldn't screw up this 'special Presidential' mission.

Upon arrival at the temporary 'Presidential Palace,' a half-buried two-story brick house with open windows revealing men in white coats tending to scientific equipment inside. Jackson waited in the car for the 'special lady' to be escorted to his car. His jaw dropped when it was none other than Sally, looking at her watch, carrying two large briefcases overpacked packed with manuscripts. She was clad in a white lab coat, under which was a high fashion dress containing the people's colors of red, yellow, and purple, with red triangles in the middle of the yellow patches.

"What's Sally wearing the Republican flag for?" Tim asked Carlos.

"It brings out the best of her, eh…anatomical features, I suppose," the normally 'I've seen women from the inside and the outside, and nothing surprises me anymore' Carlos replied, his lust-awakening eyes bursting out of the sockets.

"Or has something to do with what's in their briefcases," Jackson replied, loud enough for Sally to hear. "Which are—"

"—Scientific biomedical information that stays with us and does not get into enemy hands where they can be used against humanity!" Sally said as she proudly walked toward the car, in the kind of footwear her male compadres hadn't seen her in since their arrival in France.

"High heels," Sally barked out of the side of her mouth, her stare focused on painful agendas behind her bloodshot yet well-made-up eyes. "Which, yes, I DO know how to walk in, makes my breasts bigger, my ass rounder, and…well…another illusion."

"And we're going to the American Consulate in Barcelona because?" Tim asked as she plunked herself in the back seat, pushing Carlos out of his place there.

"Saying goodbyes to the past and a hello to the future," Sally replied as she forced a smile on her face, waving to a deeply fulfilled and relieved President Negrin. "With no time to lose. Drive."

Carlos and Tim looked at each other, each asking the other what to do about this strange woman who they both thought they once knew.

"Pronto!" she yelled out. "Por favor," Sally then pleaded, then fell suddenly into the abyss of helpless desperation.

Upon looking into the rear-view mirror while ramming his foot on the accelerator, Tim found himself looking at Sally's face. He found himself not recognizing it somehow. The right side and left both had aggressively conflicting agendas.

The American Consulate looked not too much different than it might have in the later years of the 18th century. It was when President John Adams first opened up relations between the recently hatched country called the United States and the over-the-hill but not yet in the gutter nation of Spain.

Tim Jackson, now clad in a Republican Army uniform bearing medals attesting to his courage and effectiveness under fire, noted white columns, white steps, and white walls with white people inside of them. Most prominently white was American Ambassador Claude Bowers. His thin lips, pale complexion, bulging forehead, small eyes, and a pin-stiped grey three-piece suit made him look like Dixie Democrat Woodrow Wilson's younger brother. He sat in front of a wall adorned with photographs of aristocratic and proud Confederate soldiers bearing his Surname. But the Ambassador did have a large nose, which Tim took notice of as he was led into his office along with Sally and Carlos. A nose that turned upward and winced in discomfort seeing a Black Man in Republican Army uniform, armed better than the white Marine Guards still clad in WWI Army fatigues.

"He was a journalist who's got a nose for news, Captain Jackson," Sally pointed out to Tim. She invited herself to sit down, offering the contents of her briefcase to the cautious Ambassador as payment for doing so. She tried, above all, to avoid yet another civil war in a country torn apart by ideological differences. "Yes, Captain Jackson, Ambassador Bowers has a nose for news, can smell bullshit, and enjoys breathing in the truth."

"Who has been championing our Cause in Washington for a long time with FDR himself," Carlos added, taking a seat next to Sally.

"Unsuccessfully, I'm afraid," the Ambassador related and confessed with more than a tinge of Dixie in his diction. "Who, unlike previous presidents, I had the privilege to write about. A President who can't see that this fight against Fascist Germany and Italy is a dress rehearsal for another World War," he continued, pointing to biographies bearing his name as the author. "Like visionaries such as Jefferson, Andrew Jackson, and Jefferson Davis."

Thomas Jefferson a slave owner who didn't free his slaves even at the time of his death. Andrew Jackson who owned slaves and made slaves out of millions of Injuns. And Jefferson Davis, President who called the War to end slavery 'the War of Northern Aggression, Jackson wanted to say, but didn't.

Instead, he commented on the artistry of the American-made storage boxes where the books and the other papers of importance in the office were needly packed into. Such included photos of the ambassador with President Wilson and the director of "Birth of a Nation" taken at the White House. At the premiere of the hit movie, that made heroes out of the KKK and subsequently corpses out of any self-respecting Negro who stood up for his or her civil rights.

"Are you anticipating a relocation to different accommodations," Tim said in his most accentless White diction. "Buggering outta town before da German Klansmen give you'll an eviction notice, Massar?" he spat out in mock 'Negra,' pointing to the empty shelves on the wall and then the overfilled full boxes and crates on the floor.

The Ambassador bit his thin lips, then after three deep breaths, let out what was on his mind and in his Dixie-trained heart. "Franco, our common enemy, is about to take over this whole country, as we all know, Comrades. We have to locate in France before it's too late. And my job right now, Comrades, is to get as many Americans out of Spain as possible. Those who want to get out or have the good sense to get out," he said, after which he stared Tim straight in the face. "Because despite our differences in biology, we all will be needed to fight the Fascists in the next War., which is coming…very soon."

"After we maybe beat them in this one, here?" Sally interjected, offering the Ambassador her two briefcases. "Professor Doctor Negrin's medical and scientific research files," Sally related by way of explanation. Bowers gazed through the papers with nods of admiration, respect, and intense interest.

"He and his team discovered, or maybe just stumbled on, a whole lot of what science can do for or to humanity," he noted, after which he scratched his chin, absorbed in deep contemplation. "Take them with you." he finally instructed Sally. "And, with your woman's emotional intuition, you think Juan Negrin is still the best candidate for his job as President, Sally?" Bowers inquired.

"It's DOCTOR Sally!" Tim yelled into the Bowers' face.

"And Juan is as trustworthy as they come!" Sally added.

"Hmm…," Bowers said, again scratching his clean-shaven chiseled chin. "You know him as 'Juan,' Doctor Sally Ross Whitaker?"

"Doctor 'Ross?'" Tim inquired of the woman who refused to be called anything except Doctor Sally, Comrade Sally, Sally, or Sal.

"My maiden name," Sally replied with pride.

"And Whitaker?" Carlos pressed.

"My afflicted handle, Mister and, maybe, Comrade-yet-still-Ambassador-Bowers," she confessed. "That I'll be casting off as soon as I give the appropriate parties this." She pulled out a folded-up notebook from her pocket, holding it in her hand. "Juan…eh…President Negrin…entrusted me with, well, things he said I should know about. About his personal life. His most trusted alliances and political miscalculations. And his necessary financial activities. Which, if anything happens to me, I wrote down to pass on to the appropriate parties before it's too late. Before he…dies." Tears of sorrow flowed down Sally's beet-red, angry face. "Or is…killed, Mister Ambassador."

"By you, 'Comrade Ambassador,' or your G men Klan brothers, if Nergin's colorful activities get to Red!!!?" Tim pressed.

"Or a politically ambitious fellow Comrade, or a Fascist sniper, or a dumb as shit Anarchist," Carlos interjected in a calm, sobering tone.

"Who are on the payroll of the Kings in Europe and Capitalists back home?" Tim offered. His stare abruptly got absorbed by the small library of carefully packed historical volumes and essays written by his 'host.' "As you, Mister Ambassador wrote in those books, or should have written anyway…revolutions, especially the one that was about the rights of white land-owning men in 1776, are about money."

"Not this one in Spain!" Bowers blasted at the trio of disbelieving Commie freedom fighters, abruptly breaking into a boisterous tone that exhausted him. Sincerity oozed out of his small mouth as he struggled to get air into it. With a shaking hand, he grabbed hold of a vial of pills, pushing two of them down his throat. After gaining his breath and professional composure, he pointed to Sally's notes, staring at and through the eyes of the woman holding it. "And, Comrade Doctor Ross, if you're offering those secrets about who Negrin really is and what he really did. And you want me to do something about now and write about later…I am obliged by honor and administrative mandates to defer that all too important task to others."

"Others who know Sally's last name?" Carlos interjected with courtesy and manufactured respect as a fellow 'politically connected professional.'

Bowers pulled in his lips again, sighed, and looked upward at Carlos with his own brand of respect. "Refreshing to meet a Basque who knows that the real truths in these offices are related by talking around it," he replied. The ambassador then laid his stare equally on all three expected but uninvited visitors to his current office on 'relocation' day. "But as for who the others really are, who know more about all of you than even you know about yourselves…."

"If you tell us, you'll have to kill us, right?" Sally offered.

"Yes and no," Bowers proposed, honestly, averting his eyes and real thoughts on the matter behind them. "But," he said, emerging from the silent dialog between mind, brain, and heart echoing between his large elephant ears. "You, Miss Ross, have something to live for now. That we've been taking care of to the best of our ability. Despite her father's efforts to take care of her after his inevitable conversion to the Right side of this War."

Bowers rang a miniature Liberty Bell on his desk. Two Marine Guards escorted a teenage girl into the office. Her hair was straggly, cut short on the left side of her head, shoulder length with knots on the right. Her hospital gown 'dress' was torn. Her wrists were covered with bandages stained with red blood. Her right foot was covered with shoes, her left barefoot and badly bruised.

"All of Ilene's wounds and disfigurements were self-inflicted," Bowers explained to Sally. "We did the best we could with medications from the States. But maybe with the honest and innovative discoveries from 'backwater' Spanish scientists?" He scanned the research papers from Negrin's lab. "Inspired and taught by Ramon y Cajal, more art than science Spanish researcher whose 19th Century ideas about 20th Century biology were, according to my son who works for a pharmaceutical company in Boston, never wrong. Yes…she's in better hands with your artsy docs than with our medical professionals. Who—"

Bowers' academic rant about the benefits and drawbacks of the science of medicine without an infusion of appropriate art, humanity, and humor was interrupted by Sally seeing the teenage patient's face when she lifted it up. Her eyes, as well as the brain behind them, were, like the dream of the Democratic Socialist Spanish Republic serving the people rather than the kings and capitalists were defiant, still hopeful, and...alive.

"Ilene!" Sally, released from her tight lung, rushing over to the girl, dropped on the floor the pocket notebook about Negrin's past, present, and political activities en route. All of the knots in her chest unloosened into a musical constellation of life at once as she hugged the stepdaughter she had loved more than anyone or anything. Or, for that matter, any political cause as well.

"Mom? Is that really you?" Ilene muttered from quivering lips, bite marks on them still oozing with fresh blood.

"Yes, it is, it is me," Sally exclaimed, her tears of joy merging with those of her daughter.

"Yes, the best medicine," Carlos said to his male compadres.

"Yeah, makes me think about my own kids, who have skin that was probably the color of Jesus," Tim added. "And yours too, who were cursed with ugly white skin and even uglier straight hair, Claude," the black-as-coal experiencer of War said to the white-as-snow ambassador-scholar whose life-assigned job was to write about it.

"We will all be best served if I…do pass this on to the appropriate parties," Bowers concluded. He picked up Sally's notes, carefully considering what to do with them. "Unread, of course." With that, the Ambassador placed the notes in an envelope officially stamped 'Top Secret' and placed them deep into Sally's pocket.

CHAPTER 25

It was an order given to Sally by Comrade Colonel Carlos, Comrade Captain Tim, and the most intrinsic biological law in the Material Plane—take three days off to reconnect to your soul so it will be of use to the world and...perhaps be Alive big A again. Upon waking up in the, by Spanish standards anyway, three-star mountain cabin from the first nightmare-less sleep lasting more than three hours in as many years, her eyes beheld a leather-bound parchment manuscript on the table next to the door. It contained authentic, well-preserved 15th-century Old English calligraphy. "Physician, heal thyself," she voiced as she read it. "Signed personally by Miguel Cervantes, author of Don Quixote. Dated May 4, 1596."

"Cervantes wrote in Spanish, not English, which the owner of this overpriced resort but quaint cabin conveniently overlooked," Sally heard from a voice she thought she would never hear again. "And, as any smart tourist or graduate student doing a Ph.D. in

Spanish Literature knows, or should know, Don Quixote was written at the beginning of the 17th century," a fully awake and dressed Ilene continued in a voice full of confidence as she flipped over what smelled like a cross between an omelet and pancake on an old rusty wood burning stove. "But legends related to the best intentions are more powerful than the truth presented as it really is. And just as art imitates life, when life tries to imitate art, it's a far more powerful transformation. And, who knows?" she continued, enduring the aroma passing up from the pan into her winching nose as she dared to flip the breakfast delight over to its not yet burnt to a black crisp side. "Maybe the special mushrooms Cervantes' semi-legitimate progeny, who the owner says he is, gave us for free will make us hallucinate into thinking that you or I really CAN cook something that's palatable here."

Sally self observed herself smiling so much that her face hurt. The medications she concocted and administered to Ilene the night before DID work far more than expected. Perhaps they worked on her adrenal gland, an organ which, according to Negrin, contained a wealth of hormones to awaken the body, mind, and spirit well beyond adrenalin and cortisol. But this time, Sally experienced far more than the privately experienced applause of the soul that happens when a physician is able to prevent Mother Nature from continuing to inflict disease on her least appreciative species.

Ilene's become a better me than I ever was, Sally thought but dared not say when seeing her teenaged stepdaughter put two 'authentic' Swedish-made 'Cervantes era' metal plates on the table that the master novelist had presumably used. "Or she will excel in what I did or tried to teach her," Sally said as Ilene insisted that the stepmother who rescued her from her sadistic father, as well as her own destructive instincts, sit at the breakfast table and feed her empty belly.

"To FILL your stomach this time, and not just make it less empty," 'mother' Ilene insisted. "And if you don't like the omelet I made, there's some bread, jam, and fresh fruit Tim and Carlos picked up from town. Along with sausages that, according to them, were not made from rat or mule meat. And if it was from the fat asses of fat assed Fascist prisoners or money-grubbing American capitalists, it was well cooked to kill all the toxins and contagious viruses that make you cruel, lazy, and boring."

There were so many things Sally could say now to Ilene, particularly when she saw Carlos outside the window giving her a good morning 'thumbs up' between glances at the latest dispatches from headquarters. Ilene gave a special smile to Tim as he passed by, which he returned with gratitude and cautious affection. But all Sally could come up with to the teenage girl who was well on her way to becoming smarter, wiser, and less masochistic with regard to relationships than herself was, "Yes, it IS a good morning. A GREAT morning. One with…possibilities for all of us."

"It will be if you sit down and eat, Mom," Ilene said, addressing her stepmother for the first time by a handle other than her first name. "And," she continued, after which mother and daughter both plopped their asses on the small-sized wooden chairs. They were manure and hay-smelling furnishings which, maybe, were from past centuries when men or women rarely loomed over six feet tall. Or perhaps they were merely cheap furnishings made for contemporary children from the nearby school. As a school that, once it was safe to return to, would once again be filled with kids of all ages and classes for universal free education. "Maybe you could teach me how to cook like you did back home, Mom?" Ilene asked Sally.

"With as much food as you want," Sally pledged with an open palm gently placed on Irene's forearm, just above the bandages still on her recently slashed wrists on the sixteen-going-thirty-girl. "Not just two small bites or one big whiff at the table with your father getting the rest of it to punish you for being bad. A 'therapeutic diet' to keep you thin and pretty so he could pawn you off to his buddies at the bar or G-men for boring stakeouts who…." Sally found herself falling backward into her own dark holes, some of which were self-made, as she now considered their origins, yet again. "I'm sorry I wasn't there to save you from him! All those days and nights when I was away doing what I had to do for others. And the times I was at home, and he took you away to his other homes. At times, I was arrested for doing the right thing for all of us. And trusted your father when he said that if I take care of his 'special needs,' he'd take care of your wants and needs."

Mother and stepdaughter exchanged the rest of the woulda-shoulda conversation with their own tears, hugs, and simple 'commoner' expressions. Such included the L word, the way it was supposed to be said and felt. It was interrupted by an unexpected burst of cold wind from the open window. It hit Sally's uncovered legs first.

"Spain is supposed to be a warm place," Sally noted as the shiver went up from her calves into regions 'Northward,' which had not been seen or touched with any man she really loved, not in a long time anyway. "But I suppose that's in the afternoon," she continued, easing out of the embrace with Ilene, then turning towards her oversized 'combat ready' trousers she had changed into before visiting the American Embassy.

"No! Not yet!" Ilene shouted out abruptly, with unanticipated apprehension, grabbing onto Sally's forearm. "These are warmer!" she said, handing Sally the spare pair of fatigues that Carlos left for her. "Please! It's not yet time for you to—"

"—Put on my trademark oversized trousers that make men wonder what's under them and what supersized balls I'm hiding next to my clitoris," Sally replied, gently pulling away from the step-mom-daughter embrace. She reached for the once thick and her still most favorite dungarees, which had been cleaned of blood, sweat, and mud so many times that it was as light as any summer issue fabric.

"Not yet!" Ilene screamed out, terrified, as she grabbed hold of the trousers. Such was accentuated when the young woman's gaze was captured by an antique Bavarian clock ticking down the hour to 8 am.

"What did you mean when you said 'not yet' to putting these trousers on?" Sally inquired.

"I…eh…just thought that it wasn't time for you to eh…," Ilene blurted out of quivering lips. It was with that same uncertainty and fear that Sally recalled just before it was time for 'Daddy fearest' Jack to come home. "It isn't time yet for you to…."

"Time for what?" Sally gently pressed, cautiously working her way towards Ilene. She extended her arms to the now terrified teen in stages. Ilene backed up to the wall, then slipped to the floor, then into a fetal position, locking her soul into a place where she wished she had never come out of the womb. Such allowed Sally to grab hold of the trousers, slipping them onto her cold legs.

"It's not time yet for what!!!" Sally demanded to know.

"It's only 8 o'clock!" Ilene said, somehow gaining her composure, holding Sally back with an outstretched palm as if terrified of her healing hands.

Sally put her hand into her pockets, having long known that touching someone in shell shock from the War in Spain or similar condition incurred by being at the hurting end of domestic battles at home placed the patient and person into an even deeper, darker hole. She looked at her watch. "It's already 10:30 am."

"You're sure?" Ilene said.

"Yes, I am sure," Sally assured her. "10:30 am on the tenth of July, theoretical. And that is hopefully made in Switzerland and not Germany. The clock is either 2 hours slow or 10 hours fast. But according to the world, Don Quixote didn't live in, it's 10:30 am on July tenth, 1938."

Irene was still not convinced. "Tim! What's the time and day?" Sally yelled out the window, beckoning her bodyguard, friend, and TOTALLY self-taught scholar to 'come hither.'

"Half past the past nightmares," he declared as he looked at his watch. The seasoned veteran who had acquired more internal and external wounds in Spain than in the Great War, and the undeclared ones while in US Army uniform afterward, then turned to Ilene and Sally. He reviewed events of the past in his cynical yet still somehow hopeful soul. "And it's half to a new, bright future. One way or another. If we're bold and smart enough to embrace it."

Ilene was still not certain. "Real world answer, please, Comrade Captain!" Sally insisted.

"Ten thirty-one, July tenth, 1938," Tim confirmed. "Any problems in there with that?" he inquired.

"No, not at all," Ilene said, relieved somehow. "Ten thirty on July 10th right now will do…fine." She emerged from her fetal position and then stood firmly on her two feet. More firmly than she had since Sally had escorted her from the American Consulate to a better place of healing. She attended to the breakfast table. She took into her hand a knife, slicing the bread from town into slices with escalated strength, force ease, and a full range of motion.

"Your slit wrists and…hat tendon damage," Sally noted and pointed out. "You should be more careful."

"Mind over matter, Mom," Ilene replied.

Sally took hold of Irene's wrists, her nose sensing something off with them. She smelled the red-stained bandages. "This blood…doesn't smell right."

"Maybe it does, maybe it doesn't," Ilene volleyed back. She pushed Sally away, landing the puzzled physician on her ass hard into the chair at the table. "My job now is to make breakfast," Ilene continued, violently slapping jam onto the bread. "Your job is to eat!" the somehow awakened from shell shock teenager said with a tone and timber identical to her father's. Such was made more frightening by a black cloud of 'possession' that overtook Ilene's angelic yet still bruised and battered face. A face that seemed more demonic with her unevenly self-chopped-up hair flowing up in the wind coming into the window. According to Sally's inner eye anyway, flames of hellish fire seemed to get hotter and larger with each, albeit tiny, bite Sally took of the breakfast bread.

"Good jam, Ilene. Thanks," Sally said, playing along. "I really am…hungry."

"I know, which is no problem, now anyway," Ilene replied as she imitated not only Jack Whitaker's voice but his manner of eating. She grabbed hold of the lion's share of the breakfast, placing it on her own plate. Ilene took what she wanted from Sally's plate and then filled her own pie hole. It was with the same clenched fist, slurpy mouth, and belches that 'Papa' Jack did when he was 'the breadwinner' of the family. A 'provider' who gobbled down most of the food that he said he put on the table for himself, leaving crumbs for fellow diners Sally and Ilene.

Sally wondered if there was something in the food that was making Ilene mad and herself light-headed. Her inner and now biological eyes saw even more demonic presence in Ilene than in any other human being she had experienced or treated. But there was something else that demanded attention first. "Your wrists and that blood...," Sally said, sneaking a whiff of the bloody bandage on her Ilene's wrists while holding onto them. Ilene violently whacked her in the mouth with her elbow, Jack's favorite 'mouthpiece' for ending a discussion he didn't want to continue. It landed Sally on the floor, with blood gushing out of her own mouth.

"Fake blood," Sally noted on the red-stained bandage, doing a confirmation smell and taste amidst the real blood coming out of her own nose. "For fake self-incurred injuries," she boldly shot back at Ilene, noting her unblemished wrists. "And the hair chopping you did on yourself at the psychiatric hospital?"

"With a knife, I stole from an all-heart and no fucking brains orderly that I returned back to him in the sheath between his duodenum and pancreas," Irene volleyed back between mouthfuls of grub. "The pigs in the village ate well that night. Two full human bodies for them to gorge on. Christmas came early for those porcine."

Sally considered taking on a normal conversation as to the why and how of it. But it seemed that the only way to reach Ilene if she was still in that body and mind, was through someone else. "Jack. Why did you marry me?" Sally inquired.

"I was a sadist in the service of American free market capitalism; you were a masochist who was dedicating yourself to a so-called International Democratic Socialist Workers' Paradise, who provided me with intel I needed about the Communist devils," Ilene answered, as Jack. "That I got without you ever knowing about it because you were more wise than smart and more compassionate than clever. Stupid enough not to even know when you were being followed. Taped. Photographed. By the way, we still have those pictures that can land you and your Commie Comrades in jail for ten lifetimes or fried to a crisp on the electric chair."

Sally recalled how 'the Movement' had met difficulties in progressing forward and the increased numbers of arrests of well-meaning Socialists that happened after she married Jack. Socialists he identified and found by following her when she went out. Socialist activities and members he found out about on the 'good' days when, with a warm smile and a meal HE cooked, he asked her 'how was your day?' leading her on to think that he, as a Socialist sympathizer, would promise to see that no harm came to 'those good people.' How could she have been so stupid? And gullible, thinking that Jack was an 'as good as it gets' Capitalist who could be converted to the 'give according to one's ability and take according to one's needs' way of thinking and acting, despite political affiliations. But there were more personal issues which, to Sally's mind and soul, seemed to be central to the political ones. Even in an era when political agendas were at war with each other, winner-take-all.

"Jack, why were you so mean to Ilene? When you weren't drunk on booze or power, you said you loved her," Sally inquired while looking at her stepdaughter, open to any honest answer any person or demon within her would provide.

"I did love Ilene," Jack-Ilene replied. "As a first and favorite wife. A loving wife. And business partner."

"Who you abused," Sally replied.

"Some of the time to make it seem real," came back from Ilene, as Ilene with a sadistic, confident smile of her own, far more self-assured than anything from Jack. "No pain, no gain, and me and Jack had a lot to gain by tying up you, your life, your soul and curtailing your political and scientific activities, 'Comrade Sucker.'"

"So, where's Jack?" Sally inquired after processing as much as she could and had to. "I mean in the real world."

"That big envelope in your supersized pocket," Ilene replied, pointing to Sally's trouser pocket. "It should answer…well…the question I, now that it's 10:30 am, can answer."

Sally reached into the deep, button-closed pocket. That the button had been opened, she carefully retrieved the 'Top Secret' labeled envelope containing the notebook detailing what Comrade Negrin wrote down and told her about himself, his past, and the real whereabouts of the Spanish gold reserves, that he entrusted to Sally to give to the appropriate parties, but she had mistakenly thought should go to Ilene for safekeeping and a new generation of International Democratic Socialist idealists who value freedom, service, and sharing all pies equally above all else.

When Sally opened the envelope, the notebook she brought to Ambassador Bowers that he inserted into a Top Secret envelope at the Consulate and then put into her pocket for the right recipient was gone. It was replaced by one picture that said a thousand horrifying and revealing words.

"A picture of dear old Dad, or rather my dear hubby Jack," Ilene proudly said of the photo of Jack's blood-soaked slashed corpse inserted into the Top Secret envelope she had opened without Sally's knowledge or permission. She paced around Sally like a Nazi Gestapo wolf about to devour its trapped and helpless Jewish Commie prey. Her accent relocated from New Jersey American to Hochdeutch German with each goose step she took. "You and this Revolution you came to fight for made Jack stupid and weak after he came here. His and my superiors in Washington and Berlin and employers on Wall Street all agreed that we had to end his contract. And promote me to—"

"—What did you do with my notes from and about Negrin!?" Sally blasted back at Ilene with more fervor than the Biblical Jesus had when kicking the money lenders from the Temple, or, as she envisioned, the Real Jesus had on the cross when he yelled up to his Dad, "Why have You forsaken me?"

Just as the Biblical Jesus and the Real one got when confronting betrayers of the real Faith, Ilene replied with superior Master Race condescending silence.

"Tell me where you sent my notes!" Sally demanded to know, her shaking hands clenching Ilene's throat. "Tell me where you sent my notes! Tell me, or I'll!!!"

"Kill me?" Ilene laughed back, pulling herself away from Sally's grasp. "I'll do it for you," she barked back. She retrieved a vial with German writing, and Nordic ruins on it from her pocket and moved it toward her mouth. "Sieg Heil!" she pushed out of her throat. But before she could send herself to Valhalla to set up a villa for Hitler, Mussolini, and Franco to move into after ruling six or seven decades on earth, a black hand pulled the suicide pill away from her mouth, but not before a small portion of it passed her lips and got swallowed into her belly.

"I knew you wouldn't let me die," Ilene said lovingly to Tim, taking his hand into hers.

She then turned to Sally. "And I know that you aren't going to kill me. Just like I know that it's too late for your lost and toxic cause. The intel that will defund the Spanish Republic's Revolution and discredit ALL of its leaders were passed on to my people, who used to be your people, who went…well…."

Ilene twirled her finger to the North, South, East, then West, then up in the air. She laughed louder and madder with each confident breath. Then she burst into 'Tomorrow Belongs to Me,' the Hitler youth tune which, in American English, brought so many born in the United States with German ancestry Americans back to the Fatherland and its new leader, including the Jack Whitakers. The self-administered lullaby and elixir put Ilene into a slumber that only a kiss from Adolf himself could awaken her from.

Carlos rushed into the cabin, having heard enough of what was going on to know that something had to be done and fast. He was quickly informed about the rest of the relevant details. "We do have ways of making Frau Ilene talk," he related to a disbelieving Tim and nearly catatonic Sally. "Vincent, as an Italian prisoner, snuck into a cell with her, or making an escape with her could—"

"—Get nothin' from her," Tim interjected. "Germans spit on Italians with more superior race bullshit than white sheriffs spit on darkies back home."

"Any idea who the moles are in our Army?" Carlos asked Tim.

"It's another one of her Fascist fairy tales she's telling us, so we fight among ourselves more than fighting the enemy," Tim replied. "We Lefties do that a lot."

"Yes, I know," Carlos conceded. "But—who have access to this cabin besides you and me? Maybe it would be—"

Sally somehow forced herself to fall into the abyss of learned helplessness. She pointed to the 'authentic scroll' next to the wall, presumably left by Miguel Cervantes. "Whoever wrote that," Sally surmised, listening to all of the thoughts in her aching head, trying not to quiet the whisper. "Most likely the owner of this place, who—"

"—rode into the bush with his miracle horse and headed straight North at dawn for another supply run on the way to fighting more dragons through the goat trail we got here on," Tim noted.

"Where there's a clearing big enough for an airstrip," Carlos said. "To…." He turned to Ilene, whose eyes were closed.

"Ilene, my dearest Aryan Walkerie," Carlos asked her in German in a soft, friendly voice. "It's your Uncle Adolf here. Please tell me who gave you the notes you stole from Sally. There is a special reward in it for you if you do."

From her slumber, induced by mental disease or perhaps something in the breakfast she gave to Sally to silence her into submission or death, Ilene motioned for 'Uncle Adolf' to turn around so she could whisper something into his ear. "You shaved off your mustache," Frau Ilene said, feeling Carlos' hairless upper lip with her eyes mostly closed.

"It will grow back. Now, tell me what I want to know," Carlos gently asked, as the Hitler who loved dogs and children and disallowed anyone from hunting on his Bavarian estate. "Now!!!" he barked out on the podium, screaming Fuhrer's tone, which is buried in the genetics of even the most gentle human souls. It scared Tim, Sally, and Carlos himself. But most importantly, it drove terror-fueled obedience into Ilene.

She whispered the details into Carlos' ear, then said a goodnight, 'Sieg Heil,' and went to sleep. Tim tied her legs, then her undamaged wrists up tight then put a gag over her mouth.

"We're taking this one with us," Sally asserted, angrily stumbling her way to Ilene. "Come on, wake up!" she demanded, trying to slap, punch, and plead her way into awakening SOME live human, ghost, or demon. But it was to no avail.

"Did you find out what we need to know?" Tim asked Carlos.

"Yes, she did," he said, slinging his rifle over his shoulder. "Everything we need to know right now." He placed a revolver into the palm of Sally's shaking hands. She held it loosely with shaking hands. "We have to move forward now," the Basque guerilla fighter said to the American doctor. "Now, Sally!" he insisted. "Por favor."

"Yes, I know," Sally concluded after weighing all of her options on a scale that kept tipping over every time she tried to balance it. She looked long and hard at Ilene, feeling more pity than anger, somehow. Then, with an abrupt motion, Sally pointed the business end of the weapon at Ilene's head. Then, she pulled the trigger, sending her stepdaughter to the afterlife and herself to hell on earth. "Moving forward," Sally declared as she got up to a shocked Tim and a sorrowful Carlos. "Just one question I have, gentlemen," the good Doctor said as she holstered the pistol and slung one of the Tommy guns from Tim's shoulder over hers. "Does killing get any easier the second time around?"

With that, Sally marched out the door, determined to do what was needed, whether it was right or wrong, ignoring the luxury of knowing which was what.

CHAPTER 26

There was one thing that Resort owner Fernando 'Sancho Panza' Gomez didn't realize when he rode Rocinante, named after Don Quixote's steed, into the hills. In the book, the horse could fly across even the rockiest of countryside in search of dragons to fight. In reality, the white gelding whose physique matched the Knight's outfit he wore on Cervantes' birthday for Quixote re-enactments had thrown a shoe five miles up the trail through the tree-covered mountains. Then the horse became lame two hard miles later upon finally reaching Alpine meadow, which had been used as an airstrip for rich tourists before the War and mobsters hiding from their bosses during it.

Rocinante's rider was clad as a 16th-century Knight. His ensemble included a helmet, making him a foot taller than he really was, and giant size spurs, which make his stubby size 8 feet appear to be supersized 16. He apologized to the old swaybacked sweat-soaked gelding as the horse munched on the grass.

"That maiden whose hair was chopped up by the Inquisition barbers thinking she was a witch. The reincarnation of the real Dolcinea she was. She said the fate of the free world depended on me getting a package to her friends here, with the Good Lord's speed," he confessed to the horse.

"Which we did, thanks to you."

As Carlos, Sally, and Tim arrived on dirt bikes, Gomez picked up his lance, a pike upon which was mounted a rusty oversized spear. He aimed it at Carlos, Sally, and Tim with determined eyes that were more powerful than any weapon manufactured in heaven, hell, or the 'real world' material realm in between. "Stand back, demons!" the deluded Resort owner yelled out at them through his long, white fake beard, which seemed to him to be real.

"He's mad," Carlos suggested.

"He's just been sellin' his own bullshit for so long that he's believing it himself," Tim offered as his take on the bizarre and dire situation regarding the messenger Ilene hired to deliver Sally's notebook containing Republican State secrets into enemy hands.

"And he's been drugged by the look of his pupils," Sally pointed out. "With something Irene put in his breakfast coffee and, because his horse made it this far, something she put into his horse's feed also."

"The angels took the package to the rightful owners," Sir Fernando declared.

"In what flying chariot, Good Knight?" Sally inquired, in Spanish, with an ancient accent, holding Tim and Carlos back from aiming their guns at him.

"One that had to leave here from the ground," he said. "Because," Fernando added, with tears of apology. "I shot down their flying chariot with my musket, surmising it was a giant hawk sent by the devil." He pointed his metal-gloved hand to a pile of metal behind a clump of trees, lingering smoke emerging from it. Sally, taking command of the 'interrogation,' motioned for Carlos to check out the wreckage. "I had no idea it was carrying people," Sir Fernando went on. "Kind people. Messengers who—"

"—Spoke German, were clean, polite, and wore snappy uniforms that would make you want to join them?" Carlos yelled out from the woods after examining the wreckage of a downed plane. "And had in their large chariot horses like we have?" he said, pointing to his motorcycle.

"Yes," Sir Fernando answered. "But bigger and faster ones."

"Who went where kind and noble Knight?" Sally asked the delusional five-foot-nothing middle-aged innkeeper who believed he was three feet taller and twenty years older.

He pointed to the West. "Some of them went one hundred and thirty-four leagues yonder, I heard them say. To the great waters!"

"Which means the outskirts of Lisbon, in Portugal," Carlos said with regret. "Franco's most loyal ally."

"Whose most loyal ally?" Fernando demanded to know. "And whose castle?"

"An evil one, which you will never have to be locked into, as long as you work with us," Sally assured the delusional innkeeper, who abruptly came back to 'hard reality.'

"Where am I?" he said. "And how did I get here on this horse that…I never take away from the Inn. But I remember that their leader went…yes…North, I think, maybe."

"Illusion has its benefits and can make you stronger and wiser," Sally said as she got back on her dirt bike, feeling pain in her legs and weakness in her arms. "As long as reality doesn't get in the way," she added. Upon trying to activate the bike again, it answered with a thud that degenerated into silence.

After she tried to kick it into obedience, a barrage of metal from the engine fell to the ground. She tried to lift the disconnected metallic organs off the mud-soaked ground, but her injured arms and shaking hands vetoed that order.

"You're an ace mechanic, Sally, so I heard," Tim said, picking up the parts. "You can tell me and Carlos how to fix it."

"No time for that," Carlos interjected, turning to Sir Fernando while walking his bike out of a ditch. He did a once over to be sure it would obey his commands for a long journey. "Where's the nearest telephone?" he asked the now back-to-reality innkeeper, as whatever drugs or illusions that made him Don Quixote turned him back into a commoner.

"San Franjenika," the innkeeper replied, pointing to a narrow trail leading up the mountains to the Southwest. "Assuming that the telephone wires haven't been cut."

"Comrade," Carlos ordered Tim, after which he handed him a note. "You go to this address in Lisbon. We have a package to retrieve and some real moles to dig up and eliminate. Wait for me and the others there."

"The others being who?" Sally requested and demanded to know.

"Your former traveling companions, who I should have left in France 12 months ago," he said. "Or if I gave a shit about you, would have had you sent back to America."

With that, Carlos zipped off to the Southwest while Tim offered Sally a seat behind him on his motorcycle. "And who said the man has to do the driving?" She challenged.

"The man who knows that you still have some healing to do, Doc, before you're ready to drive," he insisted.

"Yes, physician, heal thyself," the innkeeper added as a mixture of Fernando and Don Quixote.

Sally reluctantly obeyed the orders and requests, climbing behind Tim and heading West. She glanced back at the motorcycle she had driven so hard that it was unfixable. And the innkeeper, whose horse, with enough time, perhaps would be serviceable again. Thinking that 'time heals all wounds,' as long as, of course, you don't intentionally keep opening them.

"But!" the innkeeper said, shaking the cobwebs from his head, as someone other than a middle-aged resort-owning con artist milking the rich and gullible or a 17th Century Knight who bought his own, albeit magnificent, idealistic bullshit. "The officers whose plane I, or maybe a thunderstorm, shot down said they would need to see 'the Wizard' and convince him to use his magic to open the treasure chest and share it with him. Or force him to open it. "The Red Wizard" who has all of you and all of us under his spell," said the innkeeper, who knew more about the metaphysical realm AND the real one than anyone who came into his resort. He climbed atop his horse, somehow encouraging the tired steed to walk, then trot in a circle in both directions, noting that she was only mildly lame on the right front. "'The Red Wizard' whose real name is—a word that, if spoken in the wrong places, makes you…disappear!"

"Alexander Orlov," Sally gave voice to. "According to what Negrin told me and made me write down. "General Orlov, who…."

"With Nergin's approval, took 70 percent of the Spanish gold reserve from Madrid to Moscow for 'safe keeping' when it looked like Franco would invade Madrid," Carlos said, having heard the General's name. He took a U-turn back to the campground. "Yes, General Orlov, who also did horrible things to Spanish Communists who didn't want to take orders from Stalin, such as Andreu Nin, as he does to Spaniards who obey Franco, Hitler, and the Pope."

"Not anymore," Fernando proclaimed. He unsheathed his sword as the horse somehow broke into a sound trot on all legs, telling his rider with several small bucks that he would prefer to take a long-deserved rest. "According to what I saw when I confronted him in a duel. In…in…in….” The innkeeper fell off the horse, landing on his ass. He cursed the devil and praised God, so it seemed, in as many different languages as Socialists have varied ideas about how to take down Capitalism and what to replace it with. Carlos and Sally attempted to talk him back into the painful, sometimes blissful, and potentially infused dimension that lies between heaven and hell, but to no avail.

Tim walked up to the frenetically loud madman and punched him in the belly, then the face. Then he threw water into his dirt-caked face. He presented the innkeeper with a map and a pencil. “The Yellow Brick Road to the Wizard. We're off to see him,” he said. He quoted other passages from L. Frank Baum's children's book has a musicality that made Fernando recall his own childhood. “Me, the lion who needs to get his roar back, the Scarecrow, and Dorothy need to see the Red Wizard,” he related, referring to himself and his two travel companions. “Do you know where he went?” Tim asked, handing Sir Fernando a scrap piece of paper and a pencil.

Fernando let his hand guide the pencil to where the Fates required it to go. To aid in the process, he closed his eyes, then pointed the poorly sharpened pencil straight into the map to a location that felt right to him. “Yes, there, I am sure of it. As sure as I….” Fernando then fell asleep.

"A town in his imaginary universe see-able only after we eat these magic berries and mushrooms," Sally surmised after reaching into Fernando's sac of grub strapped to his Knight's belt.

"Which I know very well in my universe and ours," Carlos said, looking at the map. "Where there are better phones and more reliable equestrian couriers than in San Franjenika."

"He could be leading us into a trap," Tim offered.

"And if so, we'll somehow become smart enough to pull ourselves out of it," he said, picking up his rifle, Tommy gun, and three belts of ammo, strapping them onto his motorcycle. "We're off to see the wizard!" he stated, then sang as he zoomed off into the Northern horizon.

"Sounds like a song that someone outa put on screen, Dorothy," Tim commented to Sally, inviting her to sit behind him. "Maybe, one day, with a black woman playing Dorothy and a black guy playing the Wiz."

"We can only hope," Sally replied.

CHAPTER 27

The whereabouts of Spanish treasure, be it gold or information about the people who collected it, has always been an adventurous mystery. To steal it for your sovereign, with a healthy portion for the crew, was a pastime for pirates dating back to the time of Roman Spain. And even further back to the pre-Roman times when Celts, rich in gold and slaves to mine it, founded Lisbon and the surrounding regions of Portugal. But, ironically, the history of Portugal seemed to be the inverse of what happened in Spain. In 1933, when the democratic Socialist Spanish Republic was formed from the ashes of the dictatorial, aristocratic, and Church-serving monarchy, 'President Salizar et al. had overthrown the democratic people-serving government of Portugal. They replaced it with a right-wing conservative dictatorship that supported the rich, the Church, and 'traditional' Capitalist values, declaring Communism, land reform, equal distribution of wealth, universal education, free healthcare, and free speech as agencies of the devil.

Why Salizar's opponents didn't join the Republican Spanish Army in droves was one of those mysteries that baffled the quartet of American expatriates as well as their Basque advisor and (by more his own choice than theirs) their caretaker Carlos. Where the Spanish gold reserves really went after they were entrusted to the USSR for 'safekeeping,' as Negrin claimed in his discourse to Sally, was an even more puzzling mystery. But it was one that had to be figured out quickly so that the Fascists in Germany, Italy, Portugal, or any officially non-interventional neutral country wouldn't get it. Since in War, as in peacetime, he who has the gold makes the rules.

"And another fact," Carlos went on to the 'gang of four' American expatriates whose odds of going home on two feet were slim, and chances of returning back to their country with the idealism they had when they left were gone. They waited for the 'Red Wizard' in a three-and-a-half walled café rebuilt for the fifth time, surrounded by two mute Spaniards too old and broken to be aware of anything. Their host was a middle-aged bartender whose features suggested that it was his turn to be the 'parent' in the family.

"Just before Franco started the civil war, 'neutral' Spain had the fourth largest gold reserves in the world," Carlos continued to his compadres as he poured the 'house wine' from an old jug into four mismatched glasses. "Profits were increased beyond anyone's expectation during WWI, which may be why the committee that secretly commands all committees chose Spain as the battleground between Socialism and Capitalism, then Communism and Fascism. In an age when it's Stalin against Hitler, instead of Franco Nationalists against Negrin's Republicans."

"With us in the middle of it," still Comrade Captain John Smith replied, knowing that he was disallowed promotion due to his skin color as well as country of birth. And recalling that at Jamara, it was the American Lincoln Brigade that was sent into No Man's Land to 'test' the enemy's strength by European commanders. "But, Sally," he said to the woman who was responsible for getting this new 'special' assignment. "Why can't Negrin get back the gold Orlov snuck into Moscow in the dead of three nights?"

"Because 'Comrade Stalin,' betrayer of the Revolution, went back on the promise I gave to Juan Negrin," echoed from behind a wall in American English that had the cadence of a passion-driven Slav. But, it lacked most of the diction that Eastern Europeans and Russians retained in their speech. "And when the ten thousand boxes containing 65 kilograms of gold reached Moscow, without being stolen by Anarchists, Fascists or any non-political thieves," the 'Red Wizard' continued as he emerged from the back room and wiped off the lather on his face after having given himself a clean shave around his trimmed mustache. "Stalin proudly boasted that 'the

Spanish Republicans will never see this gold, just like no one will ever see their own ears."

Red Wizard Orlov was a tall man with a face and mustache that resembled that of Francisco Franco. His militarily arched back displayed his manly chest as he marched to the table, making no attempt to lessen the pounding of his boots on the floor. General Orlov was never out of uniform or 'off duty,' stood at the table in front of the empty chair provided for him, clad as a civilian, and continued the intel briefing, "On September 13th, a year ago, when the 10,000 boxes were loaded in Cartagena onto ships that would take them to Odessa, then Moscow, I promised on everything I held sacred to Juan Negrin that it would be returned whenever he could find a safe place for it that the Fascists wouldn't take over."

"A sacred promise made by a Communist atheist?" John Smith scoffed.

"Who is still, in the ways that matter, a Jew!" the General protested. "Who was denied promotion to being an officer in the Army when the Czar was in power despite my extensive academic training and abilities in warfare? But he was allowed to serve in my true potential in the Red Army after we overthrew the Czar at an appropriate rank!"

"And what about the Spaniards who, no doubt, went as escorts as sailors and plain clothes soldiers to help protect the gold as it made its way through Fascist and capitalist-held territories?" Sally inquired. "Who, like the gold, are maybe being kept in carefully guarded rooms in Moscow or Siberia for 'safe keeping?'"

"So, you know about that, too," Orlov said, his head lowered in something resembling shame. "Did my friend Ivan tell you?" he said regarding Carlos. "Or perhaps Igor, or Andre or, as named by his white mother when on assignment in Africa, Sasha?" he continued, pointing to Vincent, John, and Tim.

Carlos saw, across the table, Sally's shock at considering that such a proposition was true. The idea that the only four men she trusted didn't trust her with their real names was the last straw. After all, in the last 24 hours, she had found out that her virtuously bright stepdaughter was the demon seed of the devil. That her demonic husband had converted into being an Angel who was killed for such. That the boring Innkeeper, who she considered too common to be possessed by any kind of superior intelligence, was blessed as well as cursed with the clairvoyance of a madman. And that her aversion to killing had been converted into an acceptance and liking of it. "It wouldn't be the first time this week that the good guys in white hats were bad boys in black ones," she said as her now cold and distrusting eyes looked over the displaced American Comrades, who she had thought were friends. "And maybe none of you know who I really am, or were, or are working for either," she proposed to them.

"Indeed, you, madam, are someone who still doesn't know how to lie effectively or bluff convincingly," Orlov said to Sally with a smirk. "Thank God," continued the ex-Jew who broke all of the ten commandments in the service of Humanity and a Deity beyond any established religion. He pulled out the chair at the place set for him, helping himself to a seat on it. "Relax, Comrade," he said to Sally, gently putting his strong hand on her shaking wrist. "It was a joke! These companions of yours are who they say they are." 'Ivan, Igor, Andre, and Sasha' were less appreciative of the humor than Sally was, as demonstrated by their pointing the business end of their weapons at the invited 'guest.'

"If you shoot the Red Wizard, he can't help you get back your gold," Orlov said as he poured himself a glass of wine. The 'people's general' took a sip of it in the manner of an aristocrat. "Not as good as Russian wine back home, which I will never see again, but...as the expression goes, if you aren't where you are, you are no place."

While Orlov helped himself to a piece of bread, dipping it into the Spanish vino, Carlos found himself missing his home in the Basque mountains. Tim Jackson and John Smith recalled their own families after celebrating another Fourth of July without them but relished instead sharing the affections of Jenell in France, with perhaps an offspring or three bearing the surnames of Smith-Jackson or Jackson-Smith. Vinny re-visited memories of New York, where he was in line to inherit the less-than-legal family businesses but now saw them as empty prizes. Sally kept her wits about her, focusing on the present.

"The notebook Juan Negrin gave to me was stolen by the German Fascists," she told Orlov. "It named the people who could get the gold back to Spain and save the Revolution. All of whom were commanded by you. People we can contact—"

"—If you know how to resurrect the dead or dying," Orlov replied. With anger and sorrow in his eyes, he handed Sally a list of names. "Do you recognize them?"

"Yes, from what Juan Negrin told me, and I...foolishly wrote down and entrusted to...well, someone I didn't know," she said. "But...."

"I'm being recalled back too, to join them," Orlov said. "As their commanding officer who...knows far more than they do about the gold. And even more about what Comrade Stalin has done to disgrace the revolution in Spain and in Russia. Who he has killed and silenced. Including Lenin himself. Whose vision do I still serve? Me being a true Democratic Communist who—"

"Is a man who has a wife and a child or two here in Spain who you value more than any ideology?" John Smith, as a fellow academic, proposed.

"An NKVD agent who wound up on the Moscow Central Committee's shit list who maybe has a mother still in Russia?" Tim offered. "And mother-in-law, if you have the kind of marriage that makes life more happy than just 'tolerable?'"

"Or…a just a man, who maybe will make any deal with Hitler, Mussolini, or Franco to make them and YOU rich and powerful again, so you can get back at Stalin?" Carlos proposed.

"Or…all of the above?" Sally offered after the once powerful general after he hid his agenda behind downturned eyes on a face that reeked of 'vulnerable.'

"Some combination of the above," Orlov finally answered her, phasing into a blank stare. Not knowing if these Americans were good guessers regarding his background or whether Negrin or some other party informed them about his past life and future prospects. But it didn't matter. "I hear that the American racist Capitalist Ambassador Bowers, now in France, is very fond of all of you," he said with downturned eyes. He then abruptly looked up to Tim. "Especially you."

"So, you wanna become an American?" Tim asked.

"For the second time," Carlos interjected in accentless American English. "As William Goldin again? Who infiltrated American factories and other organizations over the last ten years that no one can confirm or deny? Who still speaks with a fucking Russian accent!!!!"

"Guilty as charged, Special FBI Agent—" Orlov replied, the speaking of his code name silenced by Sally's hand over his mouth. After she removed it, he turned to Sally, staring at and into her troubled soul. "Yes," he said with an understanding tone based more on intellect than heart. "Some truths we are not ready to face or deal with, but…we must, someday."

Sally looked at Carlos, demanding an answer from him.

"It's about finding out now how to get back the Gold the People's Revolution here needs," Carlos replied. "Or, at the very least, preventing it from getting into Hitler or Franco's Fascist hands."

"Or J Edgar Hoover's Capitalist serving paws?" Sally blasted back. "Or Lindberg's Nazi-loving paws? Or getting it into Henry Ford's private stash?" She named no less than 20 patriotic Americans who got rich as free market capitalists at the expense of workers who busted their backs and shut off their thinking minds in their service. "And then there is—"

"—Stalin himself," Orlov interjected. "Who…you'll have to kill, neutralize, or sneak around to get what you and the world want and need. And the gold." He got up from the table, finished the bottle of wine, then smashed it against the wall. It elicited no reply from the pair of lost behind the taverna's vacant-eyed, elderly 'patrons.' "Another bottle for my Comrades, who will escort me to France and…maybe other places!" he yelled out to the barkeep. "So we can toast the ghosts of those who died defending this establishment in the Cause of the Republic," he continued, staring at and into the blood-stained walls. "Or any other Cause they considered holy, righteous or…practical."

With that, the most clever, but perhaps not wisest, man in the Soviet Army proudly ambled to the door, sitting on the porch. He motioned with his watch and hands that the 'Committee' had five minutes to accept his offer.

"Who is he, really?" Tim asked Carlos, the only member of the posse who had reliable intel regarding the Red Wizard.

"Something we'll find out long after this Civil War, in my homeland, where I was born, is done with. And the next War is done with also," Carlos prophesied. "Maybe. But for now, we have to take a vote. For or against General Comrade Orlov's proposition?"

Tim was the first to raise his hand in the affirmative. Vinny was next, followed by Smith, and then finally, Sally. Then, after reluctance, Carlos. After which, he poured the second bottle of wine brought to the table into a mixed assortment of metal cups disfigured by bullets and schratel. "To this Mission, which we pledge, our lives, fortunes, and sacred honor."

It was with a mixture of caution and relief that Sally noted Carlos, whose love for Basque Independence within the new Republican Spain trumped all other political Causes. Or, she considered, if the Basque homeland was favored by the Nationalists, he would have no trouble changing sides, the latter being a national pastime in Spain, more popular than bullfighting.

CHAPTER 28

There were many dark days in July 1938 for the Republicans, particularly those from other countries, who found themselves now trapped within their own shrinking territories. Nationalist forces had captured every Spanish city bordering the Atlantic, along with the straights of Gibraltar. The only exit by sea and entrance route for supplies (and people) for the Republic was a small strip of coast in the Mediterranean. Entrance and exit routes by land through the Pyrenees mountains to France had diminished significantly. Thankfully, most of the French had sympathies with the Republicans, but that was as far as it went. To make matters worse, Joseph Stalin's 'cleansing' of people smarter and wiser than him at home and abroad led to fewer goods, ammunition, and 'advisors' for the Republican Cause.

It was a bit of a relief for the Abe Lincoln Brigade and other International volunteers not to be lectured to or ordered about by Stalinist 'moral' officers. Officers who wanted to turn the American volunteers into hard-line, austere Communists rather than free-thinking (and when they could be, fun-loving) Democratic Socialists. But then again, without Soviet pilots to operate planes and tanks, the instruction manuals were mostly in Cyrillic Russian rather than the Roman alphabet. Western Europeans and American volunteers with any degree of aviation experience were used.

Such was what Vincent DeAngelo saw so many times in the field as he was sent around to instruct soldiers in the art and joy of killing Fascist Nationalists. But, as Vincent knew from living outside of and, when one became a smart mobster, within the law, he who has the gold, or access to it, calls the shots. The muscle could be bought, and switch hitters like Orlov could wield enough muscle to get back some of the gold Negrin had entrusted to the Soviets. Such made it necessary for Vincent to go AWOL after being denied leave from his unit, joining up with Sally, Tim, Carlos, and John.

The Yankee quartet and the Basque band leader took it upon themselves to take the most high-ranking Soviet defector in Europe, his wife Vera, and his daughter through territory loaded with unexpected Nationalist soldiers and Franco-supporting citizens. Others who would halt their progress to France were Anarchists. Then there were the pissed-off

Republicans who were learning to hate their Russian 'benefactors' as much as the Italians and Germans.

As for what the Fascists knew, or would soon know, about where the Spanish gold was and who would be capable of stealing it back, that was another matter. "Doc Sally's a smart broad," Vincent noted to John Smith on the buckboard of the wagon carrying manure-smelling hay traversing paths between the Basque foothills leading to the Pyrenes and beyond. That fecal matter was roasted ever so gently by a warm sun that illuminated them, making them all the more visible from anyone atop the wooded cliffs above them. Smith and Vincent were clad as neutral, worn-down-by-all-sides refugees with musical instruments over their shoulders and attached to their belts, an arsenal of weapons hidden under their weather-beaten coats. "Why the fuck would Sally do such a fucking stupid thing as to write down names, state secrets, and 'personal' stuff' about 'Don' Negrin, goddammit?" the former wise guy from Brooklyn proposed to the Midwesterner who never so much as got a ticket for jaywalking.

"Because for fucking Christ's sake, still, PRESIDENT Negrin fucking asked her to!" the formerly mild-mannered white bread WASP whose now absent avoidance of using expletives had been a result of his religious conditioning, academic training, and love of using complex language rather than common vernaculars shot back.

"And why are you looking up at those hills thinking you'll have to shoot anything that moves?" Vincent shot back from the sides of his mouth. "A locked cop, or hitman shoots at anyone looking at him or her before you can get any kind of lead into what's going on in his or her gut or head." Vincent pressed, his eyes focused on the mismatched white undersized draft mare and an oversized Morgan gelding pulling the cart, somehow, in harmony with each other. "If you're going to 'scout' for snipers or recon patrols, at least play your flute like you're playing to the goddamn gods instead of trying to negotiate fucking terms of 'endearment' with ghosts."

"I don't think that's a good idea," Tim Jackson added, clad neck to toe in 'granny fortune teller' attire, complete with a large bonnet, accompanied by a whitened face and hands. Such evoked anger from his 'husband' John, or rather 'Juan.' "John's music is...well...," the camouflaged and now famous Black Major continued from atop a Polish Arab particularly chosen because of his keen hearing and usually undesired habit of jolting at anything abnormal within a hundred yards of his ever-watchful eye.

"His music is necessary!" rang out from a still mustache-bearing passenger in the cart. "But with THIS!" Alexander Orlov, clad clearly and defiantly as himself in his landmark three-piece Northern European suit, blasted out in Slavically accented English. He reached for bagpipes with his left hand in the cart, throwing them to John. With his right, he handed earplugs to his terrified gypsy-clad wife and confused daughter; the latter made to look like a gypsy son. "Announce who we are to the hills, Mister Smith!" Orlov exclaimed proudly. "That, Comrades, is an order! Charge! To the tune of Yankee Doodle, por favor!"

"The last one he'll ever give to us IF we survive it," Carlos commented to Sally, both being the 'passenger' members of the family. They were dressed in coats and trousers with more holes than cloth, complimented by mismatched footwear. He winced with pain as John enthusiastically blasted out an out-of-tune rendition of Yankee Doodle on the bagpipes that, by chance or bad luck, was recognizable to any ear it was inflicted upon. Such drove the collected trot of the horses, pulling the old suitcase and salvaged furniture loaded wagon into a sort of handleable lope. "We're supposed to be unrecognizable to any patrols in this now Fascist-controlled valley," Carlos noted to Sally.

"Or maybe we're bait?" Sally suggested. "For…maybe…them?" She discretely pointed to soldiers in unidentifiable uniforms atop the hills to the right emerging from the bush. One of them put a radio to his ear and made a call. Sally reached for a rifle hidden under a broomstick on the side of her saddle.

"No!" Orlov ordered, drawing a revolver from under his jacket and discreetly pointing it at her. "Please," he added in a civil and kind tone.

Carlos observed Sally place the rifle back under the cloth, not sure which modality of speech from Orlov convinced her to do it. He did know that Orlov was up to something dangerous and maybe necessary. And that what it was would only be detected several more miles when the foothills leading to perhaps still neutral France would become mountains. Or sooner, if Orlov didn't stop singing 'Yankee Doodle Dandy' as offkey and enthusiastically as John was playing on British Army-issue Scottish bagpipes.

By the time the sunbaked hot ground turned into high country frost, John, at Orlov's orders, had played, to the vocal accompaniment of the Soviet defector who had spent more years than he would admit in the US, every American patriotic song known to anyone West of Newfoundland. Such included Tim's displeasure, 'Dixie' and 'I am a Good Old Rebel.' Several planes flew over them, the last one landing on an Alpine plateau. Upon seeing it, Orlov commanded the 'gypsy' refugee caravan to come to a halt.

"We wait here," the Soviet defector commanded, as a General, of course.

"For what!!!?" John demanded to know; his mouth exhausted his aching lungs, yearning for twenty minutes of rest, ideally at a lower altitude.

"And for who, Comrade Orlov," Carlos inquired as his horse turned her head toward the mountains, ears fixed on something buried in the woods that was moving at a high pace. He opened his Basque eyes widely so that his metaphysical mind could see something his now logically conditioned brain couldn't understand or, as a result, see. "No," he told himself and the others. "Basajuan, Aatxe, Herensuge, and Akerbeltz drop to the ground from the clouds or climb up from rocks under the earth," he noted regarding the usually malevolent mythical spirits that had been spotted more than once by sober Basques. "I think."

"As you think accurately," Orlov said as two men in trench coats riding dirt bikes worked their way through the brush on their left flank, then appeared. After dismounting from the two-legged steeds, they walked confidently towards the assembly of refugees with upward chins. Their gait reeked of confidence that merged into arrogance. Their eyes were covered with dark lens glasses. Their heads were covered with black fedoras. Their faces were hidden with bandanas. Their intact trench coats were unblemished by dirt or blood. Their boots, polished and….

"Germans!" Carlos blasted out as he pulled out his pistols, aiming the business end of those firearms at them. *"Hande hoch!"* he commanded. *"Schnell."*

"And if they don't lower their hands, you will shoot?" Orlov said as the taller visiting 'gentleman,' with still lowered and gloved hands, smirked below his thin trimmed mustache, and the other offered a condescending eye roll. "Go ahead, please," he suggested in a soft voice lacking even the slightest tint of aggression. "You cowardly, poor, and dumb as a eunuch churchmouse, delusional, faggy Basque!" Orlov shouted out like an angry volcano blasting hellfire into a peaceful, windless lagoon.

Carlos, having had enough insults from 'higher beings' including know-it Soviet advisors, fat cat American Capitalist 'benefactors,' aristocratic flatlander Spaniards who considered mountain-raised Basques as an inferior genetic accident, and fellow penis-bearing humans who considered any man who didn't get woody inflicting harm on defenseless fellow homo sapiens as 'feminine weakness.' He fired his revolver at the feet of the arrogant Aryans, discovering that all of the chambers were empty. His jaw dropped. As did Tim, Vinny, and John, as they reached for their weapon, aiming them at Orlov as well as the unwelcomed Fascists 'guests.' They all discovered that their weapons were void of any ammunition. Sally drew up her revolver, finding the same result. The Aryans drew their weapons, which no doubt were loaded.

"You gentlemen and lady are lacking these?" Orlov said, emptying his overfilled pockets of the rounds of bullets he had removed from his escorts' firearms. "And you gentlemen have something that is of interest to me," he said to the Aryans. "A three-way split of the gold in Moscow, between us only, of course."

The tall Aryan looked at the shorter one. They had a silent conversation and then nodded in unison regarding the information they were supposed to hand over to their leaders but chose not to. The shorter gentleman motioned to the shorter one to pull out Sally's stolen notebook from under the backside of his trousers. He handed it to Orlov with a courtly bow.

Orlov thumbed through it, nodding in approval. "It's all here. And I am glad to see that the Soviets and Fascists can work together. And know that for each of us to rise up the ladder to positions worthy of our abilities, it requires a lot of money. And special handling of these kind souls," he said regarding his tired, confused, and formerly dedicated American and Basque escorts.

The Fascists pulled Lugars out of their pockets, aiming them at the Republicans.

"In ten seconds, do what you have to do," Orlov commanded the Germans. He counted down to ten with his fingers. He then walked towards Sally, whispering something in her ears while patting her ass with a playful smile, which angered all of the Republican men equally.

"And in five seconds, do what you have to do," Orlov whispered to Sally, sneaking a revolver into her clenched fist. "And don't miss!"

On the count of five, Sally emptied hot lead from the barrel into the two Fascist traitors. She screamed at the top of her lungs with mad ecstasy as blood came out of their mouths, heads, and eyes. She then grabbed hold of the pistol in Orlov's as-yet-unnamed wife's hand all too easily. After seizing her husband by the collar, Sally rammed it into Orlov's forehead.

"This is for you," Orlov calmly said, handing her the notebook that had been stolen. "All of this was the only way I could get it to you," he explained. "To ALL of you!" he related to the men. "Who…should not go to sleep and leave a stranger in charge of your camp and weaponry. Even me," he offered with a self-administered chuckle. "And if you want or need to kill me…take a vote, please. Socialist Workers' paradises become infernos if one Comrade and thief calls the shots for everyone else. And keeps all the money for himself. And can do harm to my family. Thumbs up or thumbs down regarding ME!"

Sally, her trigger finger still eager and ready to imbibe in the pleasure of sending another human being to the other side of the veil, looked to her male compadres for an answer. As if they were thinking with the same mind and feeling with the same heart, they all put their thumbs up slowly, so as to show off their prowess in bluffing to a, yes, scared for at least two or three soul-revealing moments. Orlov.

"And you?" Orlov asked Sally, who was still undecided. She lowered her gun, then tore out half of the pages in the notebook. Then she removed a lighter from the recesses of her pocket, setting the match to most of the entries. "The personal things about Negrin that the world, as it is now anyway, will crucify him and his Visions for remain personal," she asserted, gazing at the ashes with a mixture of emotions that even she could not clearly identify. She then looked at the remaining pages. "The names of who can correct this situation, maybe, if they're still alive," she said, handing the notebook back to Orlov. "I made a copy of them here!" she continued, pointing to her head.

"So, where do we go from here?" Orlov asked.

"Forward to France, then wherever we're most effective," Carlos commanded. "Without taking any more lunch or sleeping breaks."

"Agreed!" Orlov proclaimed, throwing the rounds taken from his escorts' guns back to them. "There is no time to lose and…." He finally donned the civilian refugee coat and hat assigned to him. "We have to go through the rest of these hills quietly and unnoticed," he declared. He then turned to John Smith as the former Midwesterner insurance salesman picked up his bagpipes. "And unheard, if you don't mind, please."

John reluctantly put down the bagpipes, then removed the other instruments strapped to his neck and waist, which were part of his ensemble as a refuge musician. The silence was appreciated by all two and four-legged travelers. Orlov reached into his back pocket, pulling out four passports, handing one to each of the Americans.

"Yes, the rumors about the passports taken from foreign volunteers and stored for 'safe keeping' when you enlisted in the Spanish Republican Army are true," he said as the quartet of expatriates looked at the documents that could get them home. "They were taken by courier to Moscow to be used by Soviet agents. These, I was able to get back before that happened. And as for the others," he continued, pulling out ten more. "I don't know if any of these 'missing in action' American volunteers were killed by Nationalist bullets, or those who were killed by overzealous Russia advisors after they took a day or two off, or even talked about deserting. In any case, tell their families that they fought and, perhaps, died as heroes for…hmmm."

"…Freedom?" Sally offered.

"A necessary pre-requisite for true courage," Orlov stated, contemplating more behind his eyes than any biographer could or would ever write.

With that, the ensemble of mixed revolutionary musicians progressed at a brisk trot and, when the ground permitted, slow lope into the mountains to France and destinations beyond.

CHAPTER 29

Getting back entrusted Spanish gold from a very powerful and even craftier dictator who considered it his own would take some time, some craftier thinking from whoever hadn't been killed by 'Uncle Joe' yet, and some luck. In the meantime, the 'administrative delays' of Soviet aid to the Republicans and the recall of Russian experts who were essential to their success in a war involving far more than the use of rifles, grenades, and machine guns were having an escalating effect. It was a 'now or never' affair for the Republicans. They were pushing President Negrin and the Generals under his command to go on an offensive against the advancing Nationalist Army. With an offensive that would both surprise and shock Franco's still well-provisioned yet now exhausted Army. The location for such was the Ebro River, near Madrid. A small distance ahead of the site of the decisive battle lay Corbera, the main communication and transport center for the Nationalists. Plans were that it be taken in retribution for the carpet bombing of the

Republican-held city of Guernica, the first mass killing of civilians from the air in the history of the War and the world.

After dropping off a provisionally and by necessity trusted 'Red Wizard' Alexander Orlov in Paris with Ambassador Bowers, Sally and her male compadres were sent where the War could perhaps be won on the Western shores of the Ebro, the largest flowing river in Spain. It was the, as Bowers said, 'Yorktown of the Spanish War for Freedom' where Franco and his Army could be trapped and pushed into surrender. "A gamble, but one that could win us the whole pot," he had said to the four Americans and their Basque 'godfather' as they departed with a congratulatory handshake, hug, and invisible medal he pinned on each of their chests. Or, in Sally's case, her right shoulder.

Sally could still feel that invisible medal on her shoulder as she entered the field hospital on the Eastern shore of the Ebro amidst the flood of Republican volunteers pouring into the place from which the final assault would take place against the Nationalists. Her skin was greeted by a July sun, which baked the ground even in the shade to an egg frying at 37 degrees. That is, if, indeed, there were still eggs to be had amongst the dwindling food still available, with drinkable water being a luxurious feast that was rationed carefully. Her nose was greeted by the stench of rotting flesh and coagulated blood from both civilian and military patients outside of the increasingly large indoor and now outdoor field hospital. Her ears were serenaded with the screams of the painful and the moans of the dying, to the accompaniment of shelling from cannons from the Nationalist side of the river and bombs dropped by the Italian and German pilots. All was made bearable, or at least relevant, by a voice that was all too familiar.

"Sally!" Comrade Major Juan Fernandez bolted out with a wide smile, cracking open a tired, sunbaked, prematurely wrinkled face, which now made him seem ten years older than the last time he saw her two weeks ago. "I hear you have made great friends with those in high places!"

"And low ones, both at the same time," she slurred out of her chapped lips, gazing at the patients she was assigned to treat. Her attention was quickly drawn to a 19-year-old who seemed happier than he should have, despite a nasty fresh wound in his right leg. Next to him was another relieved patient who showed off his right hand, lacking the index and alternative third-digit fingers, with a bandaged left leg. "What happened to them?" she inquired of the doctor who had been her boss, teacher, friend, and then, to the extent she allowed such anyway, lover. She strolled over to the two wounded soldiers. One of them was an Abraham Lincoln Brigade volunteer who she had rescued from shell shock with medicine from her heart and with the drug shelves she had stocked with innovative concoctions.

"They're on the list of those who are going home," Juan whispered to Sally. "Sincere souls who bit off more than they can chew when they enlisted. Useless to us now," he said with a wink. "And unfit for combat."

"Who six months ago you'd send back to the front lines so they could live as heroes and, if necessary, die as heroes," she shot back, within hearing range of everyone. "Instead of cowards who shot and self-mutilated themselves, who…should they get off their asses and hobble over to their posts unless they want to linger here and be executed!" she blasted into their faces. Sally pulled out two revolvers out of her medical kit, aiming each of them at their sweat-soaked foreheads. "Freedom or death, you two pledged when you signed up. So, which is it?"

Both self-mutilated soldiers pushed themselves up on their feet. They helped each other, limp out as quickly as they could toward the door, more terrified by the mad and now by the book doctor who, three months ago, would allow anyone who couldn't handle the war an option to leave it. "And come back here victorious behind your shields or dead over them! And that's an order!" she blasted out at them, throwing them their weapons and kit.

"Your new bedside manner, Sally?" Doctor Juan gently asked her.

"By necessity, Comrade Major," she replied. "And if I'm going to be maximally useful...I should be assigned where the killing happens instead of the dying!"

"So, you've been doing more killing than healing in the last two months?" Juan offered a diagnosis of her new condition.

"Unless we do more killing, there won't be anyone left to heal!" she replied. "And I don't take orders from any superior officer now, Major!"

"But maybe you take orders from those of lesser or no rank?" Juan replied, pointing Sally's attention to another room full of patients, mostly civilians, behind another curtain. "Who needs your services as a doctor!"

Sally considered the proposition and pondered her moral as well as military options. "Fine," she said, laying down her weapons. She slung a stethoscope around her neck and then a lab coat. "But when the offensive starts, I get to go with it!"

"How did you know about...?" Juan asked, his jaw dropped in disbelief.

"I'm a medic on the front lines, with a gun," Sally said as she tended to a wounded and highly decorated Lieutenant buried between more severely injured enlisted men and mutilated civilians.

"A medic on the front lines who will use that gun on Fascist soldiers instead of Republican deserters, or 'cowards' I trust!?" Juan pressed.

Sally put on a fake smile, then turned to Juan. "Of course," she replied, convincing the Lieutenant and the civilians around him. And maybe, Juan, if indeed that mattered anymore.

CHAPTER 30

Digging trenches and living in them did keep you alive during a war, but remaining in them was a strategy that never won a war. Unless you had more supplies, ammunition, and men than the enemy did, it was clearly not the case for the Republicans on the Eastern shore of the Ebro River. The river provided, due to its intensity of flow and amount of water, a protective barrier against Franco's Nationalists on the West side of that aqueous thoroughfare. Such were the thoughts of well-read war historian John Smith as fellow officer WWI veteran Tim Jackson informed him of the secret order passed down by President Negrin himself.

"The only defense we have now is to go on the offense," John Smith read on the 'for TRUSTED Captains and above only' memo from 'head office,' personally signed by President Negrin. He glanced at the river, its surprisingly calm surface and powerful undertow challenging any contender to do battle with it. Then, at the small metal dots atop the hills on the other side. Each represented weapons of mass destruction, and who knows how many men manned them. Those enemy positions were, according to Republican pilots flying overpriced French planes, to be re-enforced within the next 2 days. "What do you think our chances are, Tim?" inquired the still, despite exposure to the hot sun, a pale-skinned former insurance salesman whose job it was to always be on the winning side of probabilities in his former profession.

"The probability of coming out of this as heroes and examples for all fights for Freedom and Compassion that pop up anywhere else? Excellent!" Tim replied.

"And the probability of coming out of this alive this time?" John's next question.

Tim took in a deep breath. "By now, you know that the closer we get to death, the more Alive we are, big A," he offered with a confident smile.

Feeling all of the aches, pains, responsibilities, and regrets of being a middle-aged man whose soul was finally awakened four decades after he had crawled out of the womb, John pondered the matter. Upon hearing arriving motorized vehicles, he gazed from the overlook at two truckloads of newly arrived international recruits, most of them under twenty-five. "And the probability of any of us going…home?" John pressed, self-observing, his voice being soft and more vulnerable than he anticipated or dared show to the young and old men who were inexperienced, weak, or stupid enough to look up to him.

"For you, the chances of going home are…nil, nada. A snowball's chance in hell. I think," Tim informed him, handing him one of two letters from the other side of the Atlantic, postmarked a month ago. "Which is good news, maybe?"

The illegally abroad Midwesterner opened up the letter delivered two days ago, which had been steamed open. And perhaps read by Tim, the FBI, or the Soviet mail delivers who had not been called back to Moscow. Upon reading the news from what was now 'former legal residence,' John pulled back his lips with a reflective sigh.

"News about your family?" Tim gently inquired. "Or maybe wife, who you said you should have never married her. Or anyone else?"

"Who's now engaged to someone else," John related. "After seeing that picture of me, you and the others with that novelist journalist in the Iowa Tribune, and the stories about our heroic victorious exploits which…well…."

"Sometimes exaggeration is necessary," Tim said. "Legends become fact if enough people believe them."

John pondered that reality, recalling that in the 'good old (but less alive) days' before his enlistment in the Republican Army, he valued truth in journalism and speech above all else.

"But there's something else you're not telling me or maybe yourself right now," Tim pressed as gently as possible. "Like that...."

"...I'm jealous of an ex-Baseball Hall of Famer, overpaid FBI G-man, and Catholic Church administrator who dropped out of High School who is more stable, more financially secure, more handsome, and politically acceptable?" John belted out. He found himself recalling the few good times he had with his wife when he was just as dumb, secure, and accepting of American Bible Belt authority as she was. He now wished, above all things, that he could get those days back.

"And your family? Your two daughters? And your son, Jake?" Tim inquired.

"My son is over here. Fighting for...and with them," John replied, with anger, shame, and pity, pointing to the Nationalist lines across the river.

"Because he was captured and offered a Nationalist uniform instead of a spot in a Republican mass grave, or because he believed his mother's bullshit about what and who we're fightin' for?" Tim asked. "Or what his new racist clan member, Papist, conservative, Commie hating Capitalist stepdad said was the truth?"

"Yeah," the still under-muscled, thin, small-framed glasses-requiring Captain replied. He stared into space, painfully considering the worst of those agendas regarding his athletically talented offspring. "Jake always admired sports stars and wanted to be one. And…yeah…he knew how to climb the ladder to the top without having to leapfrog or fly to the summit of the totem pole."

John could feel Tim's pain more than his own. As well as the need to be practical about the present than the past. He felt Tim's large hand laying upon his about-to-be-shaking shoulder. To stop such, John placed his own palm on top of it. "But maybe the news about your wife anyway is good news," Tim offered. He pointed to Jenell, who offered a warm smile and hello to the two men as she arrived with a caravan of women. That congregation included angry ones in Republican Army uniforms, the defeated ones in black mourning dresses with matching veils, and the attractive ones in colorful dresses, which would perhaps be taken off after affirming agreements with the men whose eye sockets popped out of their heads by looking at them.

"Jenell should be with you," John said to Tim while both men waved a hearty hello to the French woman who asserted more than once that after securing a homeland for the free-thinking Spaniards in Spain, she would spend the rest of her days in France with a man who was 'bold, intelligent and caring enough to share that adventure.'

"Not possible for me to be with her," Tim replied, opening up the letter bearing an Alabama return address. "My wife got cured of her mental problems, so my daughters say that I'm needed and wanted back there now. 'To take care of the family AND to defend the cause of freedom for other non-white families,'" he read from a letter he pulled out of his pocket. "Besides." He smiled. "They started raising horses. Quarter horse Arabs."

"Steady minds with thinking spirits," John replied. He recalled his own equine companion back home who taught any open-souled rider more about himself or herself than he or she knew. He hoped Horatio, the horse he left at home, was still being taken good care of.

"In France, I heard anyway, they don't make horsemeat out of all geldings and mares," Tim assured John, after which he snuck him a fist full of money. "A wedding gift for transportation costs for Horatio, that you will accept as an order, Captain Smith!" Comrade now Major Jackson said regarding the horse John always compared to every mount in Spain who was fortunate enough be under his ass and between his gentle non-spur bearing feet.

The two men looked at and into each other, then found themselves shaking hands. Saying, somehow, goodbye to their pasts and hello to the future, both at the same time.

CHAPTER 31

Under a moonless sky on July 25, ninety boats were lowered into the Ebro River. The sound of oars of the 10 men in each of them was the only sound audible as they crossed the river without being offered any resistance by Mother Nature or 'Father' Franco. *Way too easy,* Vincent thought but didn't dare say to the nine Republicans around him who were of mixed levels of combat experience as they waded to dry land on the other side of the river. But the optimistic look on their faces, which was as bright as the moon when it was full, convinced him that maybe it WAS time for the fortunes of the Republican Army to turn around.

"It's always darkest before the dawn," the decorated Italian American volunteer, who refused to accept any official rank or wear any indication of such, said to the men fumbling around to see which direction forward was and whose weapons were whose. "Forward to Gandesa, where, by tomorrow night, we'll send a message to Franco, Mussolini, and Hitler that they have to find another country to turn into their private colony of slaves!" he declared in Spanish, trying his best to not slip into an Italian accent but not hiding at all his American diction.

Indeed, Vincent's wish turned into reality as the dark of night merged into dawn, then a brightly lit day. The 900 hungry, tired, initially scared, and minimally armed troops expanded Republican territory nearly as fast as they could walk into it. After clearing out an odd Nationalist sniper who was just as bad at shooting as hiding and stray-surrendering Nationalist soldiers as proof they wanted out of the fight, the Republicans pressed onward. They passed by abandoned Nationalist equipment and trenches. They noticed, to Vincent's expectations and rage, American-made trucks manufactured by the Ford Motorcar Company. The attempt to defuse them of any mines led to the discovery of more than one sales slip, clearly indicating that they were sold directly to the Nationalists by 'neutral' American businessmen and capitalist Moguls.

"Henry Ford is gonna get his kneecaps busted open for selling or giving away these to the fucking Fascists," Vincent pledged to his 'crew.' That crew seemed to follow him because of his experience or charisma, either one being acceptable to him. Hearing his own rumbling empty belly and sensing that the others around him yearned for any kind of lunch as much as a Republican victory, Vincent scurried up one of the hills ahead of his men. He took a look at what was going on back 'home' on the Eastern side of the river. "Hey, Comrades, lunch is on the way. Along with tanks that are carrying girls who will serve all of us dinner, eaten off of fresh plates or their naked chests!" he declared as he noted a pontoon bridge at the final stage of completion. "Andiamo, Muchachos!" he asserted in Mexican Spanish, thinking himself to be people's bandit and revolutionary Pancho Villa. That is before Villa traded in his sombrero and chaps for a fedora and suit. "Santa is delivering Christmas early this year," he told himself and the men around him.

CHAPTER 32

By sundown, the Republicans were within 25 km of Gandesa, far deeper into Nationalist territory than anyone expected. Orders from leaders who DID have official insignia on their uniforms, delivered by horsemen from the Eastern side of the river, commanded the nine hundred strong men to hold their ground.

Sally scoffed at the order. She had chopped off enough of her hair to look like a man, or if anyone looked closely enough, a Republican woman who was punished with a head shave by Nationalist troops and their clergy (who considered Republican women 'witches' who weaved plots against Christianity with their hair). She growled to her male Comrades as they received the welcome order to give their tired feet a rest. "I'm here to kill more Fascists!" the woman whose gun had killed more Nationalist troops during the advance than any man within two hundred yards of her. "Who are over the next set of hills!"

"And treat the wounded, Doc," a limping young recruit, Fernando by name, said, pointing to an older one who also still had two intact arms, made such by emergency work in the field. "Without you taking out that stray bullet that found its way into me, I'd be a one-legged paperhanger. And without you taking out that shrapnel from the mine that blew up into his right arm, my friend Pedro would have to call himself lefty."

"Some things we do because we have to," the overly old before-her-time cynic pushed out of her thirsty throat. She dismissed the compliment regarding her miracle emergency surgery performed just hours ago as an undesired and (to her anyway) valueless skill assigned to her. "Other things we do because we want to," she added, glancing with pride at the new notches on the barrel of her rifle.

By now, Sally knew she had gone mad but didn't care. It was a new kind of sanity, being constructive by assignment and destructive by choice, both to others and…herself. Such made her take in stride something from above. It was thunder, which was all too familiar to those on the ground who envisioned themselves to be under it very soon for the final relief.

Tim Jackson, from his observation post with an unshared set of field glasses atop another captured hill in the now expanded Republican front, counted the number of Italian Fiats and German bombers in the Western sky. He peered over what was anticipated to be Republican territory after the next, all things considered, easily carried out offensive. "Three of them too," he said softly to himself, after which he looked Eastward at the sky containing a paucity of French fighters. "…One of ours," he noted, being sure to be out of hearing range of the men under his command. Even more horrifying was the view he had of where the bombers were going. One horrifying minute later, he heard, from a distance, loud explosions from the East amidst loud bursts of water. It carried with it chunks of cable, metal, steel, and wood. He then turned his attention to the 22 Republican tanks and five artillery guns moving Westward on the flat.

Sargent Perez, a sixty-year, defiant-boned, five foot nothing pudgy, faced veteran of the Great War and three before that which he never talked about, approached Tim in mid-thought. He helped himself to look the terrain with the Black American Comrade Captain's field glasses, the use of which was reserved only for hand-picked officers now. "Building a pontoon bridge is easy," the former assistant carpenter who worked his way up to be the most valued construction engineer in his native Barcelona without any formal education noted calmly. "But building it in time to get the rest of our tanks, guns, and people to this side of the river, or any of us who may have to retreat back across it. Without Doc Sally or anyone else wearing a Republican or Nationalist uniform, shooting ANY of us in the back, of course. That's another story."

That story included, as Tim and Perez knew all too well, the bombing of the dam that kept the river 'tame' and crossable. "So," the most trusted sergeant in the Republican Army, who never allowed himself to be called by first name OR Comrade, said as he pulled out his sharp vintage 1917 digging shovel. "Trench warfare, just like the 'good old days, which we somehow won." He pounded the shovel into the ground. His sincerely and intensely applied action was answered by hard limestone rock saying, 'have to try a lot harder than that.' "Forward with what we have now, Tim?" Perez inquired of his military superior and good friend. "Sometimes life pushes you off the cliff because it's the only way you find out you can fly."

"Yes, indeed," Tim considered, then decided to put it into action despite orders to the contrary. He grabbed hold of his rifle and made his way down the hill. His journey down from atop Mount Sinai with the set of Commandments that would finally end this war was interrupted when the bombers turned around, dropping 40-ton 'Christmas presents' onto the solid rock-hard ground, creating flesh penetrating stones into rocks that burst into the air. Such left in their wake, for now anyway, mostly live men who would soon find out that it was going to be a long war of attrition rather than a final battle of heroics.

"We're better at enduring thirst and starvation than the Fascists are," Perez reminded Tim, pointing to the Nationalist prisoners and deserters being kept captive below. Who were almost as thin as most of the Republicans. Nationalist soldiers who bore whip marks on their backs as well as hunched over spines. Who, maybe, would be turned into Republican volunteers if they were smart? Meat for stew if everyone soon to be stranded between the advancing Nationalist Army and the river were to become…unlucky.

As days went into weeks, the bombing from above and bombardment from artillery from the reinforced Nationalist trenches continued like clockwork. The flat ground between the shallow Republican trenches that had not been blown into oblivion then became craters. After another scheduled 'request' for surrender from the Nationalists that failed to 'sterilize the valley of Communist cancer,' a private from one of the only Commie-accepting towns in Texas under Captain John Smith's command noted through dusty lips and a parched throat offered a suggestion as to the 'why' small foxholes were being converted into deep craters. "Hey, maybe the boot-kicking goosesteppin' Fascists are drilling for oil here."

"Or water?" added a former literature grad student from Queens, New York, who, if he survived, was qualified to write the kind of book that only the brave and bold would have the stomach to read. "Which is more valuable than oil right now."

"Naw, they got another strategy goin' on," added a Chicago-born teamster and Union organizer steel worker, who got more injuries from fighting strike breaking Cops and cowardly scabs than from Nationalist bullets, bombs, or bayonets. He popped his head up, staring down at the instantly created hole in the ground, which seemed to have no bottom to it. "They're trying to dig us a hole to China, thinking that we'll jump into it and not find our way back home again."

"Or a hole leadin' ta hell, don't ya know," a Dublin-born Southy Boston-raised wet behind-the-ears priest who only last month was able to grow a respectable mustache threw into the mix. "From which they can summon more demons that'll come up from the Inferno and curse us with more doubt, hardship, death, and weakness of the spirit. For which I have a cure ta fix it." Father Sean, as he insisted on being called rather than Comrade, stood atop the crater, took out the cross from around his neck, and performed an exorcism on the demons about to emerge from it. He then offered his Comrades, who were presumably fighting for a world where agnostic or atheist workers in the material realm are valued far more than clergy based on metaphysical blessings and communion. The latter was administered with sometimes editable leaves from splintered trees rather than carefully rationed lentils, otherwise known with the deepest resentment as 'Negrin's medical pills.'

John Smith, whose relationship with God was changing as dramatically as the once green and bucolic Spanish landscape around him, was the last to receive communion. Part of him still believed in God, but that Deity was still on a long lunch break. And as for Father Sean, aka Comrade Private O'Brady, it was important for the lad to still believe in something. And more important for Smith to allow that believe, as many other commanders would have chastised or shot the young priest for even THINKING of having love for God and the teachings of Jesus as part of Socialist-Communist vision. Indeed, Smith pondered the idea that perhaps Lenin's Vision of Communism could incorporate the blessings of Spirituality without the oppressive mandates of religion. As he still hoped for in this still-alive experiment in Democratic Socialism in Spain. And prayed for as well.

This time to a God who was not an old man with a big beard in the sky, but an undefinable Spirit which (not 'who') was beyond any form or attribute. Yet, when he asked that 'Spirit' why another young man had disallowed the chance to become an old one. Or when the eyes of a corpse with perhaps a terrified soul still in it spoke to him during the day before its evacuation by night. Yes, John still had within his reflexes the idea that the Deity who caused, ignored, or somehow was 'using' this suffering for a Larger Plan, God and Spirit, was still a…male. "A sadist who didn't even know he was one," he had said on more than one occasion. And thought on many others.

John had sunk progressively into 'paganism' to deal with the fates. He offered substantial portions of his ration of food to his men, and in moments of experimental desperation, the rats who found ample flesh from the dead, the wounded, and, when trying to get a few moments of needed sleep, live humans. On this day, he made another whispered appeal to Satan, daring the Prince of Darkness to emerge the most recently created 'hole to hell' for a showdown. As usual, he got no answer. He then turned to the scant forested patches in the once arbor-rich valley, daring the Basque 'messenger animals' who Carlos had seen, or believed he had seen anyway, to appear.

"Hey Akerbiltz! Basajuan And you too, Anaxe!" he called out to them. "Look at what those Nationalist bastards are doing to your forest! Where you live, or use to live anyway," he said of the black leafless collection of sticks that used to be lush forests. "Any chance you could do to them what they are doing to us?" he continued, unashamedly not hiding his madness and assertions into a whisper. "We Republicans aren't paid the kind of money Franco's goons and his Fascist advisors are paid in. But we pay each other with respect and the knowledge that whatever we do or leave behind is Right! Right?"

Though the spirit animals chose not to join the Republican Army that day, the men under John's command re-enlisted. "Right! Right!" they said again and again.

"And my final offering to you all in the service of these brave men is," Pagan 'higher than normal' Priest John continued. He grabbed hold of his bagpipes with one hand and a Republican flag tied to his rifle in the other. Overcome with blind trust in faith rather than logical reason, he set his tired feet, which were afflicted with early onset arthritis, trench foot, and/or a flesh wound that was on its way to becoming putrid, up onto a boulder leading to the highest point possible, clearly in the line of fire of the advancing and fortified Nationalist line. He delivered a music 'blow' to the enemy to reason with them with notes or paralyze them into aching between the ears that would make them retreat all the way back to Berlin. But before he could get to the second stanza of a melody which was more in his head than in the air, 'Maestro-High Priest' John found himself pulled down back into the trench which was constructed by connected bomb—created foxholes with stray rocks and, truth-be known but never told human body parts.

"It's an offering to the Basque mythological beasts this time!" John declared to the men who pulled him into safety. "I can't just sit here. I have to do SOMETHING!"

"So do we," Father Sean said. "Suicide is a sin, and I heard a court marital offense, don't ya know." After which, he began to sing the Internationale in a beautifully sacred tenor voice.

The literary grad student relieved John of his bagpipes just before the Commander-Maestro could place his lips onto the reed. "The wrong kind of music and the wrong time angers rather than soothes the Savage beast," he said by explanation. His sincerity and perhaps honesty halted John's urge to tell him that the correct quote was 'soothes the savage BREAST.'

The Texas Commie Cowboy pulled a harmonica with a bullet hole from his blood-soaked breast pocket, providing harmony to the Irish Tenor's singing.

John turned to the Chicago Teamster Union organizer, asking what his contribution to the 'intervention' was. "Some people have to do the singing; others gotta do the listening," he offered, after which he sat back and enjoyed the music. John found himself smiling and doing the same. Such got him through another day, anyway.

CHAPTER 33

The stalemate persisted for eight brutal weeks along the Ebro River. The Western bank and territories beyond it turned into a charred, blood-infused battle of attrition. Such was made worse for the Republicans by Stalin deciding that Soviet advisors and supplies were needed elsewhere. And that having more intelligence than he did was a crime punishable by doing a series of sabbaticals in Siberian labor camps or with the angels in heaven. True, the enthusiasm of the citizen soldiers on the Republic side of the WWI-style front, complete with trenches, barbed wire, and more deaths due to starvation and disease than bullets, was higher than for the Nationalists. But the trapped Republican Army and the flood of refugees in their protection were running out of food and water, and air support from Russian or French planes was a luxury of the past. The 'good old days' of being outnumbered in men and arms by two to one were now close to five to one, though no one at the time did an accurate calculation of such. Or related to the common soldier and citizen, the real numbers. But by this time, Negrin had to do something about it. An act of sanity and mercy. It was finalized on September 21st.

"Don Negrin is requesting the presence of anyone who is not from Spain at a thank you ceremony in Madrid, then sent home at his expense," 'people's Don' Vincent DeAngelo said to the men who were lucky enough to be in his crew, and lucky enough to be alive. "An offer and order, we are not allowed to refuse."

"So that someone can tell the real story about what happened here to the world before Franco's newspaper writers and filmmakers can spread their own lies about it all?" Sargent Perez asked Tim Jackson after the latter had read the news to the half of the Republican soldiers still alive in his command.

"And we, or I, can write a novel that will get me my doctorate, and that will maybe get Roosevelt to prepare for a war RIGHT NOW with Hitler and Mussolini so neither of them can take over the rest of Europe and the world?" John Smith's literature grad student offered by way of Nigrin's request to finally let the Americans and other foreign volunteers out of the unofficial contract they signed when joining the Cause 18 long months ago.

"I don't know if he's being kind, practical, or selectively compassionate," Sally said after being told about her being dismissed from military duty by the President, who she got to know as a man and possibly someone a lot deeper. "But I'm not buying his proposal to have a Church Wedding with me in Upstate New York, or as the most colorful exile in Martha's Vineyard, do a secular 'do you take this Comrade to be your lawfully wedded spouse?' ceremony for all of the cameras."

"Which he won't, Sally," Comrade Colonel Doctor Juan Fernandez reminded her after finally finding his way to the Front.

"Because you will?" Sally pressed her colleague in medical matters and, officially anyway, her boss in military ones.

Fernandez pulled back his lips, then after two professorial scratches on the beard covering his chin and three peasants 'sighs,' finally replied, "Juan Nigrin is a man who loves his country and you."

"And who loved someone else," Sally replied, feeling heartbroken. "Who he still does, I think." As others within listening range, she snatched a pencil from Fernandez's pocket and wrote it down on loose paper dropped by Nationalist planes, offering the Republicans pardon 'for their moral miscalculations and trusting the Communist devils' if they defected to their side.

"Alexander Orlov?" was about to mouth as he read the name, silenced by Sally's finger pressing on his lips.

"Sasha," she whispered into his ear. "Juan Negrin's secret lover, or Mark…who he trusted with Spain's gold reserves. And maybe his heart?"

"And your heart?" Fernandez asked.

Sally looked up to the sky, noting large flying objects driven by feather power rather than gasoline. "It belongs to them now, or soon will be," she said as one of the birds of prey swooped down for a lunch of freshly killed human meat amidst the buffet of Fascist and Republican flavors in no man's land between the lines. The woman who went through life because she had to kiss the man who almost turned her into one who went through life because she wanted to. She then punched him in the belly, landing him in the muck at the bottom of the trench, unconscious. As she headed 'over the top,' she stripped down to her blouse, then breasts, then trousers, clad with nothing but a knapsack swinging around her sashing hips while boldly singing the finale solo from Tristan and Isolde.

The Nationalist soldiers, who had probably not seen a woman in weeks and not a woman who looked like a goddess in months, popped up out of their trenches. No less than twenty enlisted men and three officers invited her to share their rations, cigarettes, or sleeping bags. She danced, then ran toward them, throwing the knapsack, then herself, in between two machine gun nests directly in front of a 40 mm artillery gun. One loud explosion later from the knapsack and ten louder ones from the ammo dump near it, Fernandez woke up. His jaw dropped when he discovered that amidst the dead bodies of at least thirty Fascists was still alive Sally, raising her right clenched fist up high, her left arm dangling from her shoulder. He rushed out of the trench at full speed to rescue her just in time for another shot from behind her to go into her head. Her body fell to the ground. It was picked up by a giant-sized vulture, which zoomed back up to the clouds faster than Fernandez's bullets could stop the avian 'trash collector.'

Fernandez allowed himself to think that Sally's Wagnerian fantasy about being whisked up to Valhalla as a reward for dying with the blood of slain enemies on her hands was real. Necessary medicine for a disease he could control no other way.

CHAPTER 34

The ceremonial thank you in Barcelona from Republican men, women, and children who would soon be under Nationalist rule for the Foreign Volunteers about to be very honorably discharged from service was something the 1500 members of the once 300-strong Abraham Lincoln Brigade would remember for the rest of their lives, along with the food.

"So, all of this 18-month adventure was about bein' invited to a barbeque," Vinny whispered to John and Tim as he smelled the generously loaded plate of meat, rice, and vegetables at the chow line as he proceeded to the 'special American food' portion of the buffet table. "With ketchup and American cheese, 'Italo American' pizza that no self-respecting person in New York would feed their dog."

"This ain't Italy," Tim reminded him.

"Thank fucking Christ," Vinny replied, biting into the offered fare, faking an 'I never tasted anything better' smile at the young Spanish woman offering it to him. "Gracias," he said to her with a bow, noting that there was a white band of flesh around her wedding ring finger. Something he had seen on too many other young women and older ones after they had lost their husbands.

"Very good," John said in Spanish of the pizza slice he was offered after taking a generous bite into a mouth that hadn't experienced a full mean in two months. "But it could be better," he said to his compadres. "If Sally was still here."

"And Carlos," Tim added. "Any of you know what happened to him?"

"Classified, I was told, by that guy over there," Vinny replied, pointing to an official-looking Republican Major.

"Missing, according to him," John added, referring to another Republican officer.

"Yeah," Tim slurred out with somber resignation. "But for now, but until we're allowed to find out, we got our own wars to deal with; we gotta back home wherever that is. And whatever it's become. And whatever WE'VE become."

EPILOGUE

No one could have provided a more profound line for the moment or the history books than Tim's 'Till we meet again in the next war against oppression' when he finally got on the truck taking him to the Spanish docks still under Republican control. One in two Americans who volunteered to fight for the Republic remained in Spain, perhaps to fight as ghosts while they awaited a more kind reincarnation.

The Abraham Lincoln Brigade was given a heroes' welcome when they arrived in New York. Two years later, when they tried to enlist in the American military to fight Fascist Germany, Italy, and Japan, they were deemed 'untrustable' by a country that considered them to still be 'Godless Communists.' But on occasion, the well-seasoned veterans came in 'selectively handy' when Stalin went to War against Hitler in 1941. Five years later, they became blacklisted after the War against Fascism was over. But they remained committed souls who, for the most part, never regretted doing what they could in a Cause they considered the Right Cause until the day of their death. A legacy for the next generation of ex-patriates who would have to fight for the ideals of their homeland in foreign locations.

ABOUT THE AUTHOR

MJ Politis departed the womb in Hoboken, New Jersey, in 1951. To make good on what everyone who supported, taught and challenged him did, he obtained a Ph.D. in physiology in 1978 which was used to publish 46 research papers in medical journals in reconstructive neurology, toxicology and cancer treatment.

He went on to obtain a veterinary degree to extend medical care to fur bearing souls in a wide variety of clinics and cultural settings across the US and Canada. In order to diagnose and cure numerous maladies of the human soul, he obtained an H.B.A.R.P. degree (human being, aspiring Renaissance person) as author of over 80 novels and novellas, as well as producer/director/writer on 27 comedo-dramatic films, which can be accessed through:

www.longriderpress.net.

He has been owned by horses for the last 40 years, currently residing in Interior British Columbia, Canada as home base, regularly commuting to New York to maintain global perspective.

Reach out to me at:

mjpolitis@yahoo.com